SWORD OF EMPIRE: CENTURION

Richard Foreman

First published 2014 by Endeavour Press Ltd.

This edition published 2018 by Sharpe Books.

ISBN: 9781799011279

CONTENTS

CENTURION

1.

Rome. 174AD.

"How's the wine?" Gaius Oppius Maximus asked.

"Sharper than a satirist's, or harridan's, tongue," Rufus Atticus replied, draining the cup. He winced slightly as he did so. "But it's still better than the swill that the quartermaster gets his hands on back at the frontline."

The two officers in the Praetorian Guard were sitting in a tavern, having recently returned to Rome from the ongoing war with the northern tribes. It was late, but the night was still young for most of the patrons of *The White Bull*. The smell of stale wine – and even staler bread – hung in the air. Men laughed, belched and cursed with an almost religious observance. Serving girls expertly weaved their way through the crowd carrying jugs and plates, trying to avoid being groped. A number of patrons shouted out their food and drink orders, whilst others discreetly whispered into the ear of the owner. They enquired about the services they could order from the serving girls which were off the menu. A lone, stray dog howled outside in the street. Maybe he was pining to be let in. Or perhaps the mongrel's howls were caused from having tasted the wine too. Cheers, jeers and the sound of dice being rolled across tables could also be heard at the back of the tavern. A couple of rival stonemason guilds sat in opposing corners. At best they eyed each other with suspicion, although looks of suspicion would likely turn more hostile after a few jugs of wine; there would be blood, rather than stale wine, staining the floor by the end of the night.

"And how's your meat?" Atticus asked, gazing without envy at the bowl of mud-brown stew in front of his friend.

"I'll let you know once I come across any," Maximus replied, with little humour. The war had cut a few more lines into the centurion's rugged features, adding to those borne from grief. The soldier's wife and two children had died from the plague. It had now been a few years since her passing but Maximus still remembered Julia, with a mixture of fondness and sorrow, every day.

"Most things taste better with wine, even this slop. Are you sure you don't want me to pour you some?"

"No, I need to keep a clear head tonight. I'm due to see the Emperor tomorrow morning. He returned to Rome this afternoon." Maximus reached again for his cup of barley water.

"I hear that Faustina has been keeping the marriage bed warm for him, through a succession of lovers... Show me a faithful wife and I'll show you an honest politician, a poor tax collector or, rarer still, a faithful husband," Atticus asserted, conveniently ignoring the irony that he himself had been the cause of many a wife proving unfaithful on a number of occasions. Indeed Atticus had not been back in Rome for even a week and he had now spent more than one night in the company of Senator Pollux's wife, Lavinia.

Before Maximus could reply a buxom serving girl, displaying both of her charms, appeared before the soldiers and addressed the younger, more amiable looking officer.

"Would you like anything else this evening?" the dusky-skinned girl, with a light in her eyes, asked as she bent over in front of Atticus and re-filled his cup. "I'm all yours," she added with a suggestive wink.

"That will be all for now, thank you," the charming, aristocratic officer replied. When he winked back her heart fluttered and her eyes lit up even more, envisioning both what was between the soldier's legs and also inside his purse. She headed back towards the kitchen, with the intention of warning off any rivals from attending to the two praetorian guards (or rather one of them in particular).

"It seems you've caught the girl's eye," Maximus remarked to his friend, unable to suppress his amusement. "Unfortunately that's the least that you may catch off her. The serving girls double-up as the whores here, I believe. It's just a shame that they can't add the ability to cook to the tricks of their trade," he added, pushing the bowl of stew away from him. Even the smattering of flies buzzing around the room stayed away from the house special, Maximus noted.

"Aye, food poisoning may be the least of someone's worries after spending the night here. We'd best not to tell Apollo about this place. Not even he'd be able be shoot straight whilst scratching his balls at the same time from a pox. Where is the lad anyway?" Atticus asked, referring to the young legionary and archer Cassius Bursus, or "Apollo" as he had been nicknamed.

"Keeping an eye out as usual. I told him that this trip would prove to be far from a holiday for him. He can eat at the barracks. We should get back ourselves. I've got an important meeting tomorrow."

Aye, but not with the Emperor, Rufus Atticus smilingly thought to himself. Maximus was due to meet someone far closer to his heart.

2.

Glinting stars studded a cloudless evening sky. A cooling breeze frequently took the sting out of the humid air. A film of grime coated the narrow streets. The fetid stench pervading the quarter the two soldiers walked through was even less appealing than the smell of *The White Bull's* famous, or rather infamous, stew. Occasionally Atticus noted the sound of a baby crying, or a husband and wife arguing, behind the shutters of the apartments he passed. Marriage was the greatest advertisement for the single life, he concluded.

"So has it all sunk in yet, being promoted to centurion?" Maximus asked his former optio. The officer furrowed his brow as he did so, noticing some graffiti on the wall which accused the Emperor Marcus Aurelius of being an "absent landlord". His tenants were dying from the plague – as he abandoned them to seek military glory. Unfortunately Maximus had witnessed similar, trite comments since he had returned to the capital.

Atticus had fought well during the recent wars with the Marcomanni and Iazyges. He had saved his centurion's life on more than one occasion too, most notably of late when Atticus had wounded himself from killing a Dacian mercenary who was looking to stab Maximus in the back. Though Maximus would miss him, on a personal *and* professional level, he recommended to the Emperor that his optio should be promoted to centurion and be given his own command. Atticus was a courageous and intelligent officer. His birth and breeding gifted him a natural authority over his men. Atticus' good humour and charm further enhanced the soldiers' loyalty towards him. The aristocratic Mark Antony had possessed a similar affinity with his men. He could drink, joke and fight with them with equal aplomb. Maximus recalled many a time on the parade ground when Atticus would merely raise his eyebrow, rather than his voice, to castigate one of their men and instil enough disappointment in the legionary to improve his performance for future drills.

"Has it been worth it, being promoted? I'll tell you once I receive the pay rise. The burden of paperwork is much more daunting than any burden of command though," the new centurion glibly replied. Despite his usual cynical and sarcastic humour, however, a certain amount of worry had begun to nag at Atticus since his promotion. He had commanded men before, but never his own. He had always been following Maximus' orders. Previously he had considered that his chief responsibility was to look after his centurion. Now he would be responsible for dozens of lives. He would have to give the order to attack or withdraw, although Maximus had once said leadership was not always a question of merely attacking or retreating. "Sometimes all you can do is just hold the line." Battles, lives, could be lost as a result of the decisions he made. Before enlisting in the army the son of the wealthy senator had spent his days counting syllables for the poetry he composed, or arranging dinners with his mistresses. As a centurion, however, it would be his duty to count the dead and arrange the rations for a hundred men. The former philosophy student, who had long concluded that life was a joke, no longer felt like laughing.

"Well if it's any consolation the paper cuts sting less than the spear tips of Dacian mercenaries."

"I'm pleased to hear it. Any other pearls of wisdom?"

"Aye. The wisest thing you can do is to pick a good optio... I know I did," Maximus expressed, with a rare fondness in his tone.

"Now usually I would think that a compliment from you meant that the drink was talking, but I know that you've not touched a drop this evening... Did you honestly think that I would make it this far though? I'm not sure if I did. I knew more about Horace than Hannibal when I first stepped onto your parade ground."

"I was confident that you'd survive and flourish. To misquote a phrase – don't give me a great legionary, give me a lucky one," Maximus replied, his dry humour returning to replace the fondness in his voice.

But it seemed that Rufus Atticus' luck was about to finally run out...

3.

Four rough-faced, well-built men appeared from out of the shadows as Maximus and Atticus neared the barracks. They seemed like former soldiers, or gladiators. Two carried spears with leaf-shaped blades, which Maximus recognised as coming from the arena, rather than being military issue. The remaining two held up wooden cudgels and sneered at the praetorians, looking to intimidate them. The largest of the thugs, his bare head gleaming in the moonlight, stepped forward, snorted and spat out a globule of phlegm at Maximus' feet.

"I'm afraid you're too late gentlemen. The tavern has already relieved us of our money for the evening. Or, to quote Juvenal, 'The traveller with empty pockets will sing in the thief's face.' You'll have to turn somebody else over if you want to get paid tonight," Atticus amiably remarked.

"We've already been paid," the chief thug replied. His voice was unnaturally hoarse. The soldiers noticed a long, grey scar running across his neck like a smirk. Such was the gleeful, cruel look in the villain's eye that Maximus suspected that he would have taken the job for the sport alone.

"By whom?" Atticus asked, slightly bewildered by the encounter.

"By the man whose wife you slept with last night," a haughty voice emitted, as a small-set, weasel-faced man stepped forward from behind the four brigands. Both Maximus and Atticus recognised the man as being Marcus Pollux, a prominent senator who worked as a senior administrator for the purchasing and storing of Rome's grain supply. A neat, black beard covered a pointy chin. A black wig sat upon his head – with all the grace and attractiveness of a dead crow, Atticus thought. His eyebrows were painted on, which apparently was the latest style among the political classes. Stupidity never goes out of fashion it seems, the newly promoted centurion further mused. Pollux was also wearing a garish purple cloak, fastened with a large, bejewelled brooch which almost out-sparkled the night sky.

"Here I was thinking that we would need to guard against spies and enemies of the state, rather than jealous husbands, when we returned to Rome," Maximus said to his friend, rolling his eyes a little in exasperation. The soldier caught a whiff of the senator's perfume as he moved forward to address Atticus – and Maximus would have preferred the smell of the watery stew to that of the florid scent currently assaulting his nostrils.

"One of your fellow officers told me that you would be heading back this way. I'm here to teach you a lesson."

"Hopefully it won't be a lesson from you in how to dress." Atticus eyed up the four men who accompanied Pollux. He sensed that this was not the first time that the senator had used the men to help teach someone a lesson. Rufus would have fancied his chances with Maximus alongside him should there have just been two of them, but the extra numbers and the two spears gave Pollux an advantage. The squat but muscular figure to his left either possessed a pronounced sneer or hare-lip. Saliva seemed to be forming in the corner of his mouth. Perhaps he was salivating over the impending violence. The thug directly in front of him looked Egyptian. He gripped his spear tightly and kept switching his gaze between Atticus and Maximus, as if weighing up who he wanted to attack, or kill, first. He wore a chain around his bull-neck which appeared to be decorated with ivory – or human bones. The large, bald-headed brute in front of Maximus wore a grey tunic which was either stained with wine, or blood. He jutted out his chin and offered a challenging gaze at the stone-faced soldier before him. Finally, to Maximus' right, Atticus took in a man with flat, porcine features. He tapped his cudgel against his thigh, impatient to get the beating over and done with – so he could spend his earnings on women and wine.

"If you turn back now and go home I won't cripple your men, or break your nose," Maximus flatly remarked, with all the raw contempt that a soldier should have for a politician.

"Either you're incredibly arrogant, or incredibly dumb. Or both," Pollux, his face screwed up in disdain, replied. The senator looked – and spoke – as if he had a permanent bad taste in his mouth. Perhaps his bitterness was borne from never being elected to the consulship. Marcus Pollux had never felt rich or respected enough for his liking. He had beaten his wife (or rather he had one of his attendants do so) to punish her for disrespecting him. For turning him into a cuckold. Now he would instil fear and respect into these two lowly soldiers. "Nobody touches my wife."

"That may well be the reason why she strayed," Atticus drily pronounced. He recalled how Lavinia had said that her husband slept in a separate bedroom to her. His tastes were for young boys and girls. Increasingly the senator would spend his nights at a high-class brothel for the political and merchant classes. The establishment both fed and satisfied his appetites. Atticus had seduced Lavinia at a party. Later that evening, when he climbed up the balcony and knocked on her shutters, she willingly let him in. Lavinia opened up her heart, and other bodily parts, during the remainder of the night.

The senator's face reddened in either anger or embarrassment. He was just about to give the order to unleash his human mastiffs upon the soldiers when Maximus' voice sounded out in the half-light.

"Apollo, take out the two spears."

A second or so after the centurion gave the order an arrow thudded into the thigh of the thug in front of Atticus. The arrowhead cracked the man's femur.

The archer had positioned himself on the balcony of a nearby house, having shadowed the officers since the tavern. Before entering the capital Maximus had warned the legionary that they might run into trouble at some point. Cassius Bursus had kept an eye on the situation and readied an arrow, awaiting an order from Maximus.

The Egyptian brigand let out a curse but Apollo barely registered the sound as he fired off his second arrow. The spear-wielding assailant in front of Maximus swung his head about, searching in bewilderment and fear for the enemy archer. The ambushers had been ambushed. The sound of the zipping shaft in his ear was quickly succeeded by a biting pain in his hip. The hoarse cry of pain the former gladiator let out was cut short through Maximus stepping forward and punching him in the throat.

The squat brigand's face with the hare-lip was now twisted in terror, rather than in a sneer, as he ran down the street, anxiously looking behind him for an arrowhead glinting in the moonlight. He melted into the darkness, nearly as quickly as his courage had disappeared.

The thug with the porcine expression had his features flattened even more as Atticus' fist crashed into his face. His cudgel clattered to the ground, shortly before he did.

The Egyptian whimpered on the cobble stones. The hulking, bald-headed brute who had led the assailants was also prostrate. He looked up at the impassive soldier, baring his teeth in either fury or agony.

Marcus Pollux's red face was now pale with fear as the centurion walked towards him. The senator's wig was comically askew. He thought about offering the soldier some money, in order not to harm him. He could also make a promise to Rufus Atticus that he would not stand in his way should he wish to continue to see his wife. Pollux opened his mouth but for once the verbose senator lost the power of speech.

"If I ever see your face again you'll need a mortician rather than a surgeon. You understand?" Maximus said, or rather growled. Pollux nodded his head vigorously in reply. The fringe of his black wig now reached down over his painted-on left eyebrow. Without warning the soldier jabbed Pollux in the nose, breaking it in two places. The weasel yelped and did his best to remain conscious at the sight of his own blood. "That's just to prove to you that I'm a man of my word, which is more than can be said of most of our politicians."

4.

Morning.

The shimmering heat dried Maximus' throat and made his palms sweat even more as he strode up the Palatine Hill towards the Imperial Palace. Rome sprawled out beneath him, a great tapestry of wealth, poverty, vice and (to a lesser extent) virtue. His heart beat faster and he was filled with a sense of anxiety – and happiness – not because he was due to meet the Emperor, but rather he would soon be seeing *her*.

Aurelia.

They had first met three years ago. The Emperor had ordered Maximus to escort Aurelia and her brother Arrian to the front. Their father was a German tribal chief. Marcus Aurelius asked Arrian to petition his father to support Rome in the ongoing war with the Marcomanni. The tribal chief betrayed Maximus, but his son and daughter didn't. Arrian died helping Maximus and Atticus escape. Aurelia chose to leave with the Romans, rather than remain with her father. Initially she had borne resentment in her heart towards the soldier when they first met. Aurelia was a Christian and she had viewed Maximus as her enemy. During their time together Aurelia grew to admire him, however. And to love him. She had returned to Rome whilst he remained on the northern frontier but they regularly wrote to each other. Maximus thought her witty, compassionate and beautiful. He still thought about Julia, but did he now think even more about Aurelia? She didn't ask anything of him and he didn't promise her anything in return – but they both envisioned a future together. A rare daydreamer's smile lit up the praetorian's usually stony expression. The guards at the gates of the palace almost didn't recognise their superior officer, due to the strange grin on his face.

The Imperial Palace may have been considered two buildings in one, the Domus Flavia (which contained the state function rooms) and the Domus Augustana (which served as the Emperor's residence). The palace had originally been commissioned by the Emperor Domitian. Domitian was a ruler with few virtues, but at least he had the good sense to employ someone with good taste to oversee the project – the architect Rabirius. As Maximus walked through the gilded state rooms and corridors of the Domus Flavia he was as awestruck now as he had been when he had first been posted on guard duty at the palace. The decor was a perfect marriage of grandeur and taste. As Atticus had commented to his fellow centurion recently, "Too many people nowadays equate money with taste... They believe that the apogee of art is to shock, or be new or different... But there's nothing new under the sun, including vulgarity... Even Rabirius would fail today to create something memorable if directed by the wife of Rome's leading charioteer, for instance. Have you seen her? You can take the girl out of the subura, but you can't take the subura out of the girl it seems... If only the rest of Domitian's reign had been as impressive as the Imperial Palace though... Even Martial didn't have a bad word to say about the design."

Maximus walked over polished marble floors of differing colours and geometric patterns, past gleaming black basalt statues of Aeneas, Scipio Africanus and Augustus – and more than one of Domitian himself. The centurion had long lost count of the number of dignitaries he had seen grow wide-eyed and slack-jawed as they took in the building's opulence and feats of construction. Many had been humbled into considering that the palace was home to a deity rather than man – indeed when sitting in his throne room Domitian would demand that he be referred to as "lord and god", and the largest banqueting hall was named "Jupiter's dining room". Yet Domitian knew he was all too mortal, as evidenced by the number of white marble walls throughout the palace – which the Emperor had asked to be installed so that he would be able to see the reflection of any potential assassin behind him.

Domitian could often be found sitting in the Aulia Regia, his throne room, during his reign. Marcus Aurelius, however, spent more time in the adjacent hall of the basilica, where he heard and made judgements on legal disputes. Maximus recalled how the Imperial Palace would have once echoed with the sound of harems and feasting, yet during guard duty at the palace the praetorian had only ever heard raised voices during passionate philosophical debates, which were fuelled with watered down wine and fresh fruit.

*

The smell of freshly baked bread and freshly cut grass filled the nostrils of Galen, the Emperor's physician. The slightly grating sound of wooden practise swords clacking together on the lawn filled his ears, as two teenagers played soldiers. Galen pursed his lips and tried to stoically endure the disquieting noise. He concentrated on the peaceful sound of the fountain in the background and tried to lose himself in thought. He was due to give a lecture later on in the week. Galen began to compose mental notes on his subject – and also jokes, at the expense of his backward looking rivals in the medical profession.

"Thank you again for saving him," the Emperor remarked with heartfelt gratitude, as he fondly gazed upon his son fencing with a friend on the grass. Galen wordlessly nodded his head in acknowledgement of the comment and took in his friend, Marcus Aurelius. His beard was greyer and the crow's feet were more pronounced around his tired eyes. Yet still intelligence and nobility were enthroned in the Emperor's features, Galen judged. If only he could say the same for Commodus, his unruly son. A month ago Galen had indeed arguably saved the boy's life. Commodus had returned from his afternoon at the wrestling school with a fever. The tonic that a respected physician prescribed only seemed to weaken the patient and Commodus' condition became critical. Thankfully Galen was able to treat the patient in time. He realised that the tonic was the cause of his weakened constitution, rather than a cure for it. Ignoring the protests of other physicians Galen ordered that the patient should be given a solution of honey and rosewater. By the end of the week Commodus had recovered his strength – and was even demanding that he should be allowed to commence wrestling again. Faustina had written to her husband with the news that Galen had saved their son.

In saving the boy though, have I damned an Empire?

The Emperor judged his son to be "spirited". The more objective physician, who had spent more time with the boy than his father, had other words to describe him. Commodus shared his birthday with Caligula. If only that were the only thing he had in common with the tyrant, Galen lamented. Commodus was a handsome boy, despite occasional bouts of sickliness. His bright eyes could flash with both charm and spite, depending on his mood. His hair was blond and curly. He had of late been given to sprinkling flecks of gold in his hair, to give off "an aura of the divine", as the teenager had pretentiously remarked. Galen could almost forgive the boy's wilfulness and vainglory – he was a young man after all – but what troubled him was the cruel streak which ran through the son of the Emperor. Commodus actively enjoyed bullying and humiliating playmates, staff and officials alike. He scolded people and encouraged any audience present to laugh at his victims. He was fond of decapitating animals – dogs, goats, ostriches – for sport. Alarmingly, for Galen, Commodus frequented the coliseum far more than the lecture halls. He seemed obsessed with violence, particularly gladiatorial combat. He had recently taken to dressing himself up as a *secutor* gladiator. He would also stride about throughout the Imperial Palace carrying a club and wearing a lion skin. Galen recalled the incident a few days ago when an official had called him "Commodus, son of Marcus Aurelius" – to which the petulant youth replied that he wanted to be introduced as "Hercules, son of Zeus."

"Excuse me," Marcus Aurelius remarked to his friend, as he got up from his chair and left Galen in order to attend to a clerk who wanted the Emperor to glance over some documents.

Galen gently shook his head in disappointment, as he continued to think about Commodus – Rome's future. Galen was shaking his head in disappointment in relation to the Emperor too. Few people knew Marcus Aurelius as well as Galen. The physician admired his friend as a ruler, philosopher and even warrior. But as a father he had failed, or was failing. Marcus professed love for his son – but love is blind, Galen judged. The Emperor had provided an abundance of good tutors for his son but, to use a Christian analogy, he had been throwing pearls before swine. Galen appreciated his friend's wisdom and insight on all manner of subjects, but Commodus was his Achilles heel. That very morning the Emperor had tried to convince Galen, or more so himself, that the youth was slowly but surely improving in regards to his studies. He quoted Hesiod, to bolster his belief.

"If even small upon the small you place
And do this oft, the whole will soon be great."

In his reply Galen was tempted to quote Plutarch, "One should not put good food into a slop-pail," but the usually forthright physician desisted.

A short, shrill yelp sliced through the air. The boy Commodus was playing with cradled his hand and ran off, whimpering, as the Emperor's son crowed and lifted his wooden gladius aloft in triumph. Commodus had impetuously – and viciously – struck his opponent on the hand before the fencing bout had officially started. Galen shook his head, more vigorously, in disapproval and disappointment. The boy had, consciously or not, committed the offence while his father's back was turned.

The adolescent's eyes lit up on seeing the centurion Gaius Maximus walk towards him. Commodus preferred gladiators to soldiers, but Maximus' fame preceded him. The teenager had met the officer during one of his visits to the frontline. The visit had coincided with a number of victories and the army considered the boy a lucky mascot. Perhaps he would have the soldier serve as one of his bodyguards when he became Emperor, Commodus thought.

"Maximus! Did you see me fight just now? Did you see me win?" His voice was high-pitched, demanding, aristocratic. The centurion had heard such voices a hundred times before in the army, as scions from great families gave the order to attack whilst sitting upon their expensive horses behind the shield wall.

"I saw everything, Commodus."

"One day I will be proficient enough to fence with you and the finest gladiators in the arena," the youth proudly said, puffing out his chest as he did so.

"I look forward to it. I'll make sure to wear a gauntlet for protection, however," Maximus replied, looking at, or through, the figure in front of him. He recalled again the scene at which the Emperor and his son had attended the flogging of some legionaries on the northern frontier. Marcus Aurelius had looked on in sorrow, wincing slightly with each lash – whilst Commodus had taken everything in with a sense of glee in his eyes, wildly grinning with each crack of the whip.

Commodus felt a small shard of shame under the glare of the centurion, which he resented. And he resented the common soldier daring to talk to him in such a manner. He was the future Emperor. He was Hercules, the son of Zeus.

Gods should punish transgressions rather than show mercy.

Commodus thought how the praetorian would need more than just a gauntlet one day to protect him from his wrath.

Whoever's not for me is against me.

5.

As the Emperor attended to various officials and correspondence Maximus spoke with Galen. The physician admired the soldier, for his loyalty and professionalism. Galen had been witness to how integral Maximus had been in helping Aurelius to contest and win the Battle of Pannonia. Pannonia had been a significant victory (the enemy hadn't crossed back over the Danube to attack Roman settlements since) but it had not ended the war. Indeed the battle had just been the beginning of the bloodletting. The Marcomanni and other northern tribes had learned the lesson of entering into large scale, pitched battles with the Roman army. Yet the conflict was still not devoid of bloodshed. Skirmishes and ambushes broke out in forests and marshlands as the Emperor pursued the enemy. Few days passed without Maximus having to draw his sword. Even the most visceral nightmares could not rival the horrific scenes the soldiers experienced during the day. Hands grew calloused from carrying shovels, as well as swords, as legionaries buried the dead – their friends. The wetlands were home to more diseases then even Galen could classify. But still the army advanced and won minor victories. The Emperor out-manoeuvred his enemies through both feats of arms and diplomacy. He proved ruthless in dealing with the Iazyges, a nomadic warrior tribe who sided against Rome. Although the Iazyges did not possess a homeland Marcus Aurelius vowed to wipe the barbarians off the map. The constant campaigning took its toll on the Emperor and Maximus however, both physically and emotionally. Maximus, like many a soldier before and after him, drank to take the edge off things. During the journey from the north to

Rome the centurion could still taste a tang of blood in the air. The smell of burning settlements – and corpses – still filled his nostrils. Only the thought of Aurelia brought the weary soldier some genuine peace.

As important and welcome as the news was from the north that Rome was continuing to win the war Maximus was more concerned with the battle that the Emperor had asked Galen to fight at home – against the plague. The scourge hung over Italy – and beyond – like a storm cloud. Some Christians preached that the disease was a punishment, sent by the one true God, for Rome's paganism and sins. Some critics and graffiti artists had also recently proclaimed that the plague was a punishment for the Emperor prolonging the war in Germania – albeit the plague pre-dated the start of the conflict by several years. Facts rarely got in the way of certain politicians and dissenters spouting nonsense, however. What was true was that the plague was decimating the Empire: farmers, soldiers, merchants, slaves, aristocrats, women and children. At its worst the soldier had heard that the disease had killed up to two thousand people a day in Rome alone. The storm cloud rained on one and all. The centurion had all too often passed through settlements along the Danube and Rhine where the dying outnumbered the living. More soldiers had fallen to the disease rather than to German spears. "Decimation" was underestimating the scale of the pandemic, for the scourge killed more than one in ten. But the one enemy that Maximus wished to defeat the most he couldn't even bring to battle. A cure wouldn't bring back his wife or children, but it might just bring him some consolation to know that the disease would no longer widow or orphan others.

The worry lines deepened, like scars, in Galen's brow when Maximus asked the physician about the pandemic. Over the years Galen had witnessed all manner of horrific injuries and diseases. He had dissected all manner of animals. Blood, puss and infections had been the meat and drink of his career. Yet the plague was different. The physician had found it increasingly difficult to remain objective in the face of the disease. Whereas many people had had their faith shaken in the gods in the face of the plague, the pandemic had shaken Galen's faith in the power of science – and himself. Science dictated that diseases should have cures, problems should have solutions. But the plague appeared to laugh, contemptuously, at such mantras.

Word had spread that the Emperor had charged the famous physician with finding a cure – and many people in Rome called the scourge "the Plague of Galen". Galen remembered a scene from many years ago when, after having dinner with the Emperor, Marcus Aurelius had ordered the scientist to find a remedy. Or rather his friend pleaded with him to do so, after cataloguing the extent of its destruction whilst burying his head in his hands. It was the only time that the physician had ever witnessed the stoical Emperor break down and cry. Ironically, to combat his sorrows, Galen threw himself into his work, following one of his own maxims: *employment is nature's physician, essential to human happiness.* He worked tirelessly, recording symptoms and experimenting with treatments – all the time exposing himself to the deadly disease.

When walking the streets in Rome now the physician, who had once basked in his notoriety, often wore a cloak and hood in order not to be recognised. Some had looked at him with pity in their eyes over the past year, appreciating the burden the doctor must have had to bear. Some stared at him and then averted their eyes in disappointment. But worst were the expressions of hope that the physician encountered from people and patients, when they believed that he would be their saviour.

It was in hope more than expectation when Maximus asked the physician if he had made any breakthroughs in finding a cure. Galen's grief-filled sigh articulated his answer as much as the words he spoke.

"Unfortunately the only breakthrough I've made is that I believe we are dealing with not one, but two, plagues. And each disease is as fatal – and incurable – as the other... But let us not ruin this sunny afternoon with too much gloom Maximus. Let us speak of other, better, things. Have you taken the opportunity to visit Aurelia since you have been back in Rome?" Galen remarked, eyeing him knowingly.

The usually stern looking soldier suddenly appeared a little surprised and awkward – with blushes even colouring his suntanned complexion. Maximus knew that Aurelia and Galen had kept in touch since their mission together in the north all those years ago. But how much did he know about Aurelia's feeling for the praetorian and, conversely, his feelings for her?

"How has she been?" Maximus asked, unable to suppress the light in his eyes when he thought of her.

"Aurelia keeps herself busy. She invested the money that the Emperor gave her wisely. Yet she ploughs most of her wealth back into the clinic and refuge she set up for the poor... I still occasionally see her, every few months or so. She is a remarkable woman Maximus, accomplished, well-read and good natured. But there's something missing in her life I think... Despite locking herself away she still has plenty of would-be suitors knocking on her door, admiring either her beauty or wealth..." Galen smiled inwardly, thinking of how, whenever he saw Aurelia, she would always steer the conversation towards asking after the soldier. Galen also hoped that the centurion would take the hint when he had said that there was something missing in the young woman's life.

I may not be able to find a remedy for the plague, but at least I can hopefully cure two people of their loneliness.

"Should *you* knock on her door, though, Maximus I'm sure that Aurelia would let you in."

6.

"Let us hope that we can draw out the fox from his burrow. Rufus' plan is sound and based on reliable intelligence. I'm not sure how triumphant he'll feel, however, if his plan works and his suspicions prove correct," Marcus Aurelius evenly remarked. He wore a plain, simple white tunic. Maximus thought he looked more like a school teacher than an Emperor, military leader or demi-god. After bidding Galen farewell in the garden the Emperor had invited Maximus into his study to discuss their real purpose in returning to Rome. Events and intelligence reports suggested that the Emperor possessed a new enemy, one who lurked in the shadows rather than facing him on the battlefields of Germania. There was increasing evidence of someone spreading propaganda throughout the Empire, to soldiers and civilians alike, in the towns and in the countryside. It labelled Marcus Aurelius a warmonger, more concerned with personal glory than the welfare of the people. The pamphlets and graffiti also accused the Emperor of ignoring the plague, or even causing the scourge through his devotion to philosophy rather than religion. The gods were angry, they reasoned. Falsehoods, like weeds, grow quicker and are harder to eradicate than truths.

"Rufus will do his duty, even if it indeed turns out that his father sits at the centre of the spider's web," Maximus replied, still worried for his friend should it turn out that Pollio Atticus was the snake that Rome was clutching to its bosom.

The two men sat at the Emperor's large cedar wood desk. Copies of Plutarch's *Lives* and the teachings of Epictetus sat open on the desk. Various correspondence also covered the entire surface of the aged but still sturdy piece of furniture, which had once belonged to Augustus. Some letters were due to be read, some Aurelius was writing himself. Maximus also noticed that the Emperor was still composing his book of meditations, which he had worked on in an ongoing way whilst campaigning. Soldiers, ever conscious of how orders could get them killed, learned to read upside down and Maximus took in the lines the philosophical Emperor had recently written.

The soul becomes dyed with the colour of its thoughts.

"If I were a Tiberius or Nero I could execute Pollio on a mere suspicion or whim. Should Pollio be Emperor too and he suspected that I was conspiring against him I've little doubt that he would execute me in the blink of an eye. But I will need proof, the law should be adhered to, in regards to bringing any enemy of the state to justice. The best revenge is to be unlike him who performed the injury," the Emperor said sagely.

Maximus here less sententiously thought to himself how he would put the venerated statesman to the sword, rather than put him on trial, should he prove to be guilty. Weeds must be cut down.

"We should soon know how guilty or innocent Pollio Atticus is. Rufus and I will be attending a party he's hosting tomorrow evening. We also believe we have some strong enough bait to lure him out into the open."

"Be mindful you do not fall into any traps yourself Maximus. There are more serpents in Rome than in any marshland back on the northern frontier. At least the Marcomanni line up in front of us in a shield wall, when trying to kill us. But in Rome you are more likely to perish through receiving a dagger in your back, by your best friend."

"How were things on the frontier when you left for Rome?"

"Our enemies are still drawing away from us, like a retreating tide. Yet there's wisdom in their cowardice. Our supply lines grow ever longer – and thinner. We need to recruit more cavalry units. I have staff due to meet various horse dealers while in Rome. Horse dealers and quartermasters together in the same room, however, may make even politicians and tax collectors seem honest," Marcus Aurelius posited, sighing in exasperation. The increasingly grey-haired Emperor then looked up at the map of Germania on the wall and narrowed his eyes in concentration. "I fear, Maximus, that my reign will see more years of peace than war, despite our recent advances."

"History will treat you well," the centurion said, sincerely and determinedly. Maximus had spent enough time by his Emperor's side to consider him a good man. Marcus Aurelius had shared many of his soldiers' privations and led from the front. He was a just legislator and keenly felt the losses that the war and plague had had on Rome.

"It's not History that I have to look at in the mirror each morning though, unfortunately. History doesn't have to write letters to the families of fallen soldiers. Posterity and praise will not reduce the numbers dying from the plague this month. I've been unable to save so many, Maximus. Black thoughts blacken my soul."

"You have done your duty."

"But it's not been enough. We both know that Rome is dying. I sometimes feel that I've been more of an undertaker than an Emperor. But I have no wish to live to bury you Maximus. You too have done your duty by Rome. But you also owe a duty to yourself, to be happy. I do not want you to return to the frontier with me. Rather than soldiers, I will soon need more diplomats and bureaucrats on my staff, to draw up peace treaties. You should remain in the capital. My wife's collection of dresses and shoes is probably worth more than anything else in the Empire; I dare say I will have to build a new wing for the Imperial Palace in order to house her wardrobe. You can guard it by day and at night I want you to return to a wife and family... Find some peace Maximus, that's an order."

7.

The afternoon sun massaged rather than stung Maximus' skin. He heard the faint sound of birdsong in the background, behind the spluttering cacophony of curses and the other noises that Rome daily threw up. Even the smell of ordure, which usually stained the air of all but the Palatine Hill, was absent from the streets as Maximus made his way to Aurelia's house. He had had Apollo launder his best tunic. He had also paid Atticus' barber, rather than using "Chopper", the barrack's barber, to cut his hair.

Although the praetorian seemed half caught in a dream, with his mind's eye fixed on the woman he was visiting, Maximus couldn't help but notice the number of beggars and amputees – ex-soldiers – in Rome. The Empire often honoured the dead from wars and glorious battles, but too often the people forgot about the living, those who returned from conflicts. Ex-soldiers were often looked over for jobs. Few recognised a legionary's virtues and usefulness when he no longer wore his uniform. After reading Maximus' letter about soldiers who had been wounded and had returned to Rome, having taken up drink rather than employment, Aurelia had made a conscious effort to hire veterans and amputees for the businesses she had a share in. She did so out of reasons of productivity, as well as compassion.

*

Atticus regretted having eaten at the barracks, given the endless dishes of meat, fish and fresh fruit being offered to him by the slaves at his sister's house. Occasionally Claudia would sample a tiny amount from one of the plates but then with a wave of her hand she would dismiss the attractive looking slave boy or girl. The brother and sister sat in a richly furnished triclinium. Sunlight shone off various ornate marble statues. The newly promoted centurion sunk into one of the sofas, half swallowed up by the soft cushions. Although he had grown up in similarly opulent and privileged surroundings the scene now felt slightly unreal to the soldier.

"I'm pleased that you can attend the party tomorrow evening, mainly for selfish reasons of course. You can help keep me company, Rufus, as I look down on half of the guests in attendance. I'm joking – it'll be much more than just half the number of guests. But father will be happy to see you too," Claudia remarked, popping a small cube of honey-glazed pork into her mouth. Her long legs were tucked beneath her as she sat on an adjoining sofa. She wore a shimmering turquoise wrap over an elegant, silk stola. The graceful woman would have to make sure that her lover, who would be visiting after her brother, did not crease her new dress in a clumsy show of passion.

"Hopefully he'll set aside for me just the few moments that he methodically apportions to all of his guests at his parties. If father sees me for any longer than that then I fear I'll start looking down on him – and him on me – again," Atticus replied, half-joking at best.

"Will we be seeing Maximus at the party too?" the woman asked, nonchalantly. She even sighed, as if already bored by the whole event. Claudia had long admired her brother's superior officer though, both for his physique and also his character. Maximus was unlike all the would-be suitors who had tried to court Claudia over the years. He neither sycophantically held her up to be a goddess, nor treated her like a high-class whore. She had known him when he was married and hoped that, after Maximus had mourned his wife, they could become friends – or something more.

"He would rather prefer engaging with a dozen German spearmen than engaging with some of father's friends, but yes he'll be attending. And what of Fronto? Will this be one of the few evenings in the year where you suffer his company?"

"No. Thankfully my darling husband is away, taking care of some business. He is no doubt taking care of his new mistress also. She is the wife of a tax collector, of all things," Claudia remarked bitterly, ashamed that her husband had chosen to have an affair with someone so lowly in rank. "She lacks wit, style and taste. She's a social climber, who will forever be stuck on the first rung. In short, they are perfectly matched and no doubt they make a happy couple." Claudia slyly smiled at her own joke – and from looking forward to seeing Maximus again, unencumbered by the chaperone of her husband.

*

Maximus' heart beat even faster than when he was about to advance into battle. He wiped his sweaty palms on his tunic, took a deep breath and knocked on the door. The house was tucked away in one of the nicer, quieter parts on the Aventine Hill. Fruit trees hung over the walls and vines and myrtle criss-crossed along the side of the property.

A shutter opened, and then, after the unlocking of several bolts, a fresh-faced maid opened the door and the visitor was welcomed in. The house was clean and modestly furnished. The centurion noticed a few landscapes on the wall, scenes from the *Aeneid*, which Arrian had painted years ago. Maximus was unsurprised to see a well-stocked library as he was led down a corridor to enter the triclinium, which opened out onto a pretty garden – where Aurelia was waiting for him.

It had been three years since the soldier had last seen her. Three long years. But the three years, through their letter writing, had been filled with hope, affection, friendship and – hopefully, now – love.

*

"I will duly pick out which women are available – and those who are married – at the party. Although the one can often still mean the other," Claudia said, smiling into her wine cup. She had missed talking to her brother these past few years, if nothing else because she thought him as equally immoral, or rather amoral, as herself. Most of the women she knew were either untrustworthy, or prudes. As for the men in her life they usually had only two things on their mind, sex and money. Yet with Atticus she could also discuss literature, politics and poetry. With Maximus too Claudia felt comfortable with being herself – that self who she wanted to be.

"How do you know that I have not fallen in love – and promised to be true to someone? Maybe now I'll go no more a-roving?"

Atticus broke into a grin before even finishing the sentence, unable to keep a straight face. His sister, having drunk a couple of cups of wine, let out a burst of unaffected laughter. It was the first time Claudia had laughed in such a way for a long time. For all of her lovers, she often felt desperately lonely and unhappy. The more women envied her, the more she wanted to be someone else.

"I know you as much as I know myself brother. You get bored too easily to promise to be true. You're fated to be a Tantalus or Sisyphus – forever unfulfilled. I'm just surprised that you have been wedded to army life for so long."

"Maybe I'm no longer the epicure and wastrel that you once knew." Atticus grinned not as he spoke this time.

"I'm not against being proved wrong, but the older I get the more I sense than no one ever really changes. When you take off your uniform you're still you underneath, Rufus. No amount of Virgil or Horace, or being in the presence of our divine Emperor even, can edify some people. No one can outrun their shadow, even if they run away and join the army to fight barbarians on the northern frontier. By the time we reach our twenties we are fully developed. I could not now grow a moral bone in my body, even if I tried to," the woman said, with as much sadness as satire in her voice.

"Maybe I'll get to surprise you. But more so, I hope you get to surprise yourself one day."

*

Although Aurelia had barely slept the evening before, thinking about her meeting with Maximus, there was life rather than tiredness in her expression. She rose from the bench she was sitting on to greet her visitor. Her long, glossy black hair was pinned up on her head. She wore a simple white linen dress that was fastened by a black belt. Her figure was demure and athletic at the same time.

"Hello," she said, beaming as warmly as the afternoon sun and tucking a couple of stray hairs behind her ears which had fallen down onto her face.

An array of flowers bordered a lush green lawn, brightening and perfuming the air. But for Maximus, they paled in comparison to Aurelia's gleaming jade eyes and fragrant scent. The birdsong sounded sweetly, but not as sweetly as her voice. If his heart had recently pounded like he was going into battle then Maximus now felt victorious – or defeated by her loveliness. Now, finally, he felt like he was home.

He stood and gazed at her, dumbly, for a moment or two. Making sure she wasn't a dream. Her sun-kissed features had softened, rather than hardened, with age.

She's even more beautiful now than she was three years ago...

She took him in, an alloy of honour and strength. The usually tough-looking soldier was smiling like a teenager. She sighed, in relief and pleasure. Her prayers had been answered.

He had come back to her safely. Three years. His letters had been the highlight of her weeks. Aurelia wondered again if Maximus had heard her whisper those words in his ear in the forest, when they were escaping from her village. She had said them because she feared she might never see him again. But she also said the words because she meant them. Maximus hadn't responded at the time, nor had he said anything when he had escorted her back to Rome.

Maybe I whispered the words too quietly.

"Have you come from your meeting with the Emperor?"

"Yes."

"How is he?"

"Tired, melancholy, overworked. But he's still good humoured and good natured. In short, he's the same as ever."

"He's the best of Emperors I think, but in the worst of times... I have seen some of the graffiti and read some of the propaganda attacking him... But the people are devoted to him."

Maximus was tempted to reply that the people may prove to be as faithful to the Emperor as Faustina, but desisted.

"I believe that they would love him all the more if they knew him," he loyally stated.

I fell in love with you, the more I grew to know you.

*

Claudia shooed away the slave girl approaching her with a plate of sliced, spiced apples. With the same gesture of her hand, however, she beckoned over the boy cradling a jug of wine.

"The frog-faced senator I'm about to see is unlikely to intoxicate me, so I may as well have another," the mistress of the house exclaimed, after seeing Rufus raise his eyebrow at her drinking. Wine helped her forget, lose herself. Her father had introduced Senator Piso to her a week ago. He had asked her to lunch with him the following day. The evening after that, when his wife was absent, the aged senator invited the attractive, urbane woman to dinner at his villa. Claudia left the following morning, while the would-be consul remained snoring, or rather croaking, in his bed. Pollio Atticus sometimes used money or veiled threats to win influence, but at other times he employed other assets at his disposal. Claudia could not now remember a time when her father hadn't pimped her out to his friends – or enemies. The young girl had obeyed him all those years ago because she respected and loved her father. He had instilled in her the importance of family. She also enjoyed the attention she received from some men. Beauty was power. "You are worth a dozen cohorts my dear," her father had proudly exclaimed, after she seduced a wealthy merchant to help the family win a mining contract. Claudia had once felt that she was in competition with her brother to gain her father's attention and respect. But now she envied Rufus, for having escaped his baleful influence. Her eyes were red-rimmed with sleeplessness – and tearfulness – behind her make-up. She had suffered so many miscarriages that she could no longer bear children, she believed. Her gown hid the bruises on her arms from where Piso had roughly held her from behind.

Everyone has a uniform, or a role they must play.

Yet for once Claudia would willingly do her father's bidding. It wouldn't be business, but a pleasure. The previous evening Pollio Atticus had instructed his daughter to seduce Gaius Oppius Maximus.

*

Maximus and Aurelia sat on the bench together. A breeze rustled the leaves of the tree hanging over them. Sunlight melted the wisps of cloud overhead like snowflakes. Laughter entwined itself around the birdsong. A young slave girl watched her mistress as she stood by the door, ready to attend to her but at the same time giving the couple their space. The waifish teenager, Helena, had been orphaned by the plague. Aurelia had met the girl during a visit to the refuge for the poor she had set up and had decided to employ her within her household. Helena smiled at seeing her mistress interact with the centurion. She had never seen her laugh or be so animated – and enamoured – with a man before. The smile on Aurelia's face reminded the slave girl of the expression she had worn when she had ventured out into the garden to read – and re-read – the letters the soldier sent her.

"Galen tells me that you have invested wisely with the money the Emperor gave you after the Battle of Pannonia," Maximus said. "You've earned the old physician's admiration it seems, which is easier said than done."

"Galen also told me that I have you, as much as the Emperor, to thank for the capital he gave me. I wanted to thank you in person, which is why I've not expressed my gratitude before. You could have kept the money for yourself, no?"

"Let's just say that I thought you were worth investing in. And I was right. The right people are seeing the fruits of your labour, from what Galen says."

Aurelia, glowing from having earned Maximus' admiration, was about to quote from the gospels to explain herself but she suddenly thought of something the Emperor had said, whilst she had sat near him at a dinner one evening.

"The only wealth which you will keep forever will be the wealth you give away."

Their eyes were locked on one another as their hands crept forward, until they laced their fingers together. Three years. Three years thinking about the words she had whispered into his ear, in the forest. So much remained unsaid. When

Maximus escorted Aurelia back to Rome all those years ago he believed the timing wasn't right in telling the young woman how he felt. Did he even know how he felt? She had been in mourning for her brother and he had still been in mourning for Julia. But three years had been a long enough wait. It was now time...

Maximus gently squeezed her responsive hand and leaned towards her. Aurelia's body trembled a little, but not in fear. A slight splash could be heard from the pond in the garden as a koi carp broke the surface of the water, fleetingly scanning the scene. Helena's eyes widened in shock, and happiness, as she saw Aurelia lean in towards the handsome centurion.

"I love you too," Maximus whispered in her ear, finally responding to her words, three years after having first heard them.

She drank in the words and the sight of his contented face. He squinted in the sunlight, and at her beaming countenance.

"What do we do now?" Aurelia remarked, innocent, curious, excited. The virginal young woman had never been with a man before. Maximus had been worth waiting for though.

"Well, after I kiss you, I'm going to tell you how the Emperor has decided that I should remain in Rome, rather than journey back to the frontier. I'll also tell you how much I want to make a life with you..."

Marry you.

8.

Evening.

Shadows danced upon the wall. The flames from the fire by Pollio Atticus' desk flickered in his cold eyes. He smoothed the sides of his oiled, silvery-grey hair and adjusted his toga. Too many politicians forsook the traditional garb of political office nowadays but the would-be revolutionary was also a staunch traditionalist.

Finely crafted mosaics, depicting scenes from Rome's war against Carthage, decorated the walls and floor of his private chambers. Busts of Vespasian and Seneca sat either end of a large desk, which had once belonged to Marcus Crassus. The seller would not have dared lie to the buyer about its provenance. Pollio Atticus also wore a gold ring that once belonged to Pompey the Great and carried a dagger within the folds of his toga that Marcus Brutus had reportedly used when assassinating Caesar. The statesman collected antiques, as well as people.

Atticus continued to finish off the sentence he was writing, not wishing to lose his train of thought, before looking up to address Chen. The powerfully built Chinaman served as Atticus' bodyguard, as well as an agent, enforcer and assassin. Chen had just returned from a visit to the gladiator school, situated just outside of Rome, which his master owned.

"How are the men? Has the delivery of arms and equipment arrived?" Atticus asked, scratching a speck of dirt off his toga. The senator had recently purchased the school as a cover to train a small force of mercenaries. Pollio Atticus intended to destroy the city's grain supplies by burning down the large wharf on the Tiber which stored the surplus.

"The fastest way to get to a man is through his stomach Chen... Aurelius once preached that poverty is the mother of crime, but more than poverty hunger will cause a man to despair and revolt... Rome will look to its Emperor to feed it, but he will be unable to do so," Atticus had slyly remarked to his agent several months ago. Through bribing Marcus Pollux Atticus had also secretly been able to buy up the surplus of grain from the east. The crisis in the capital would quickly spread to the rest of the Empire – a plague of civil unrest. When the time was right, the senior statesman would step in as the saviour of Rome.

Cracks were already beginning to form. Atticus need only prize them open some more. There had recently been food riots in Capua and Ostia. Dockers had downed their tools in Brundisium. Atticus had composed most of the propaganda himself. He targeted mothers whose sons had been conscripted and farmers whose workers had been taken from them by the state to feed the Emperor's appetite for warmongering. Christians, those "great haters of the human race" as Tacitus had once described them, needed little encouragement to dissent. Atticus' pamphlets encouraged them not to pay their taxes and not to serve the false idol of the Emperor, quoting scripture to support his arguments. At the same time he criticised the state for not collecting taxes efficiently or fairly – the people should not suffer at the hands of a corrupt bureaucracy. After composing such propaganda and giving his agents their lines, to perform like travelling actors, Atticus would then meet with his fellow senators and remind them of how the Emperor demanded "contributions" from them at the beginning of the war – and then state that Aurelius was intending to tax the rich again to help pay for his vain-glorious campaign.

The people deserved strong leadership. When in power Atticus would put the whole of the northern frontier to the sword, as Caesar had put down the rebellion in Gaul. *Corpses can't revolt.* Similarly, to deal with the plague, he would cut off any diseased limbs. He would quarantine and terminate the contagious without mercy. He would at first promise the people a cure though, to give them hope and gain their support, even though they knew none would be found. *The world wants to be deceived, so let it.*

Atticus believed he could garner the support of half the senate, when the time came. The other half would follow like sheep. Or he could win support through bribes and threats. If need be Chen would make a senator an offer that he couldn't refuse. Yet the wily statesman had no desire to challenge the Emperor openly. *He who wields the dagger never wears the crown.* Atticus intended to be the power behind the throne. *Real power.* He had selected his challenger to Aurelius years ago: Avidius Cassius – an ambitious, popular commander who possessed the support of numerous legions in the east. Atticus had paid off Cassius' debts years ago. The only debt he owed now was to the senator. Atticus had also introduced Cassius to Faustina a year ago – and nature had taken its course. The two were now lovers. Even the Emperor's wife would want to see an end to Aurelius' reign.

Pollio Atticus was sage enough, however, to know that the Emperor's reign was far from over. He still retained the loyalty of the majority of the army, especially the legions who had served under him in the north. The "Absent Landlord" had also returned to Rome. The food dole had increased to celebrate his homecoming – and games had been organised. *Bread and circuses.* Frustratingly Atticus was still in the dark as to the Emperor's true purpose in returning to the capital. Unofficially he was visiting his wife and family, during a break in the campaigning season. But something was amiss. Far more than Faustina and Commodus Aurelius had been spending time with various senators, rebuilding his power base. Atticus' spies had also reported that the Emperor was spending an inordinate amount of time with the scientist and self-regarding quack, Galen. *Why*?

His frustration boiled over the previous evening when the senator had dinner with his young mistress. He had raped her, as he had done to her mother a decade ago when she had served as his lover. The "Augur", as Atticus was sometimes called for predicting and shaping the political wind, needed to know what his enemy was up to. Yet he soon would know, he smilingly thought to himself. His agents had informed him about how close the centurion Gaius Maximus was to the Emperor – and that the praetorian had returned to Rome shortly before his master. And so Atticus had instructed Claudia to get close to the soldier. *She's Circe*, *Cleopatra and Calypso all rolled into one*. Men became as garrulous as Nestor in her company. Like so many others before him Maximus would be boastful and indiscreet, looking to impress his guileful daughter. *He'll talk – pillow talk*.

"The men are ready. The equipment has been delivered," the Chinaman said. Chen had often drilled – and disciplined – the small force personally. In order to cement his authority and "inspire" the mercenaries he had murdered half a dozen insubordinates, or slackers, during the course of their training. He had also culled the men for pleasure. The humourless Chinaman only felt amused, or alive, when killing.

"Have the other targets been finalised for the coming month?" Italy, not only just Rome, needed to bleed and burn for the people to rise up and the Emperor to fall. After destroying the grain supply in the capital Atticus would deploy his secret, private army elsewhere – in dozens of towns. They would incite violence, destroy food supplies and spread propaganda throughout the peninsula, motivating others to do so too. The Emperor would be powerless to stop things – and a powerless Emperor is no Emperor at all.

"Yes. All is set." Chen smiled, revealing a set of sharp, blackened teeth. He smiled out of pride for fulfilling his orders – and in anticipation of bloodying his sword again.

9.

Dawn.

Steam wafted up from the plates of freshly baked bread and sizzling bacon on the table in the tavern, *The Trojan Pig*. Rufus Atticus and Cassius Bursus delved into their breakfasts, finally coming back to life after the long night beforehand. The centurion had treated his legionary to an evening in a high-end brothel.

"The night off will put a smile on his face," Atticus had explained to Maximus, back at the barracks.

"Just so long as it doesn't put a rash between his legs," the centurion had replied, before declining to join his friends.

The young archer grinned, wolfishly, from the taste of the fatty bacon and from the memories of the previous evening.

"The redhead told me that she wanted to see me again, that I was a good lover," the soldier eagerly exclaimed, still intoxicated by her beauty and still smelling her exotic perfume on his skin.

"Just be content to lose your money rather than your heart to her Apollo," the centurion said from experience, wryly smiling from recalling his own rakish teenage years and his first visit to the establishment.

Cassius Bursus nodded to convey he understood, but he still believed that he was special to her. She seemed genuinely impressed that he could be so young and yet serve in the Praetorian Guard... and she even told him her real name.

"Did you ever lose your heart to someone when you were my age?" Apollo was always keen to know more about the enigmatic officer's colourful past, although the more he got to know Atticus the more he seemed contradictory or unknowable. Perhaps there was a love affair in his past which explained everything.

"I used to be a poet. I lost my heart every week to a woman, especially to the ones who spurned me. There were some girls who lost their hearts to me however – especially when they saw the size of my purse."

"Your father is wealthy, no?"

"As wealthy as sin, as a Christian might say."

"And you chose the army over your inheritance? Never mind about losing your heart, did you lose your mind?" the legionary said in good humour, mopping up a pool of grease on his plate with his bread.

"I chose a life serving in the army rather than serving my father... Despite being a rake and gambler when I was young I still felt I wasn't sufficiently morally depraved enough to go into politics."

Atticus' father loomed large in his thoughts again. More than anything he needed to know if he was guilty or innocent of crimes against the state and if he was responsible for trying to kill Arrian – and himself – three years ago. As the Emperor had said, "I need evidence, rather than coincidences." Atticus thought that, if he had been all powerful, he probably would have also been all paranoid and looked to prosecute and punish his enemies on the basis of mere suspicion. Caesar's famed clemency was insincere, but astute, in the days of the Republic. The centurion hoped that Aurelius' genuine clemency wouldn't prove his undoing.

Atticus recalled how, as a child, saying the name "Marcus Aurelius" was tantamount to swearing in his house. "The imperial family are a bunch of bastards, illegitimate... All that should matter to you is this family... The blood which flows through our veins flows through the history of the Empire as much as the waters of the Tiber flow through Rome," his father had drilled into him, on more than one occasion.

And so when Atticus had announced that he would be joining the army – and serving the Emperor – Pollio criticised his son for betraying the family, as well as for making an idiotic decision. The powerful statesman wasn't used to being defied. Nor did he wish to suffer the embarrassment of having a son serve in the army as a lowly infantryman.

"You are breaking your mother's heart by the way you are conducting your affairs."

"I rather think that mother's knowledge of your extra-marital affairs has broken her heart," Rufus had argued back.

It was at this point that Pollio Atticus, enraged that his son or anyone had dared speak back to him in such a way, raised his hand to Rufus. Yet the young man flinched not and, witnessing the formidable look in his eye, the senator struck his son not.

"I know you. You will soon come running back to Rome."

"It's because I know you – and that I don't wish to turn out like you – that I'm running away."

Honey-coloured sunlight poured into the tavern, as did a few other late night revellers and some market workers, grabbing themselves a hearty breakfast before starting their shifts. Atticus yawned and promised himself that he'd catch up on some sleep, as well as paperwork, before attending the party that evening.

"Rufus Atticus, as I live, breathe and shit," a rough voice called out. "I thought a vicious barbarian, or a jealous husband, would have caught up with you by now."

The centurion grinned and shook the hand of Milo, the landlord of the tavern which was situated close to the barracks. The praetorian had spent many a late night and early morning in *The Trojan Pig*. Atticus took in his old friend, a former legionary. His nose was still as red as the wine he served. He looked a little older, however, as his serving girls seemed a little younger, than he had when the soldier was last in the capital. Atticus introduced the infamous owner of the establishment to Apollo.

"Apollo, this is Milo... He's the best landlord in the district. His cups and jokes may not be clean, but his girls are..."

"You'll do well to listen to this man here lad. He'll keep you out of trouble, or if you're lucky he'll lead you into some," the sanguine veteran said, laughing at his own joke. "So what brings you back to Rome?"

"Family business," Atticus wryly replied, after a short pause.

10.

Dusk glowed like the orange embers of a dying brazier. A dry heat filled the summer evening. Lanterns, burning olive oil and a musky perfume hung upon trees all around the garden. The rustling of silk dresses competed with the sound of rustling leaves. Rome's senatorial and plutocratic elite strutted on the lawn like peacocks. Attractive slave girls and boys, wearing specially designed tunics braided with gold, carried endless silver trays of wine and food and served the guests. Couches, next to marble and bronze tables, were dotted about over the grass along with ornate sculptures. A juggler, a poet, a sword swallower, a fire eater and a brace of wrestlers entertained a small crowd towards the far end of the lawn.

Husbands and wives, or sometimes husbands and courtesans, conversed in hushed tones. Some laughed with their fellow guests – gossiping about those who were absent or uninvited. More business and policies would be enacted this evening, during whispered conversations, than would be during a month of discussions in the Forum. Pollio Atticus, his toga flowing in the wind, gracefully and purposefully moved amongst his guests (when people weren't forming a queue to catch a moment of his time), bestriding Roman society like a colossus. He remembered most people's names, although those who he got wrong were too scared to correct him. His eyes gleamed like the lanterns. He smiled as much as the courtesans. With the Emperor absent the former consul was the brightest star in the firmament for the guests to flutter around like moths.

"You look nervous," Atticus said with an amused, rather than worried, look on his face. He and Maximus walked out into the garden, dressed in their uniforms. Maximus surveyed the scene before him and took a deep breath, remembering how much he disliked attending such events. There was no one he wished to buy – or sell himself to. The only society he had needed in the past, when serving in Rome, was his wife and children. The people here didn't like him and he didn't like them. *But duty called...*

"I'd rather be a new recruit again, about to step out onto the parade ground for the first time," the centurion replied, exhaling in exasperation. The officers already drew a number of looks. Most of the aristocratic statesmen eyed them up, looking down their aquiline noses at the soldiers. A few of their wives, however, raised their eyebrows in appreciation – and smiled suggestively.

"You look more like an actor who's about to go on stage for the first time."

"Aye, unfortunately I've the urge to step out and throw rotten fruit at my audience though," Maximus said, scrunching his face up in annoyance as a flamboyantly dressed senator eyed him up too – and smiled suggestively.

"Well, like it or not, it's time to say your lines. Seize the day, to quote Horace."

"I'd rather seize a jug of wine."

"Well if it's any consolation I've reason to be nervous too. I suspect that there are a dozen women in attendance that I've slept with over the years – and *they're* in attendance with their husbands."

"Duty calls."

Maximus looked forward to a time when Aurelia, rather than duty, would be calling out his name.

*

As Atticus went off to speak to his mother Maximus fended for himself. People and trays of food swirled around the awkward looking centurion. He gripped the handle of his sword, either out of habit or to intimidate anyone from approaching him. Maximus beckoned to a slave girl and asked her to fill his cup – again. He wished he could be back in Aurelia's garden, his head in her lap, as he lay on their bench. The afternoon sun and her fingers had caressed his face. She had read Virgil to him – the battle scenes, but her voice had still been soothing. They had spoken about the future, something the soldier hadn't dared to do for some years. Aurelia had mentioned how she had bought him a ring, a gold band, but she that would give it to him after she had had it engraved.

"Centurion Maximus, it is an honour to have you here," Pollio Atticus remarked, parting the officer from his fond memories of his afternoon with Aurelia.

Maximus was tempted to reply that it was an honour to be in attendance, but he knew he wasn't that good an actor. Pollio was used to playing the part of the gracious host, however, and he smiled and made charming small talk. With the raising of a finger and nod of his head he also directed half a dozen attendants whilst giving the impression that the guest he was addressing was the most important person in the world to him.

"Have you met my daughter, Claudia?" the statesman asked, moving aside slightly to allow the soldier to take in his daughter in all her glory.

"I have." Maximus bowed his head slightly, but was unable to take his eyes off the captivating woman in front of him. Claudia was so alluring that it almost hurt some men to look at her and not possess her. Half her hair was pinned up, whilst the remainder hung down in delicate, shiny ringlets. An elegant satin dress, shimmering from the light of a nearby brazier, accentuated rather than disguised her lithe figure. Her eyes, lined with kohl, were fine and narrow and seemed to curl upwards in a smile.

The soldier had been long starved of such beauty, Pollio Atticus considered, as he watched Maximus feast his eyes on his daughter. She would render him speechless, until it was time for him to talk.

"It's nice to see you again Gaius. Thank you for keeping your promise and taking care of Rufus on the frontier." Claudia's smile dazzled as much as her silver and pearl earrings. Maximus remembered the last time he had seen her, three years ago, when leaving to journey north. She had asked him to look after her brother. Maximus could also remember the first time he had met her. It was at a lunch. He could even remember some of her witticisms and what she had worn. The soldier may have been happily married at the time, but he wasn't blind or dumb.

"My family owes you a debt. If ever you need anything, my door will be open to you Maximus. Let me start by having my daughter take care of you, as you must please excuse me. My arm isn't nearly aching enough from shaking hands with people and my voice isn't nearly hoarse enough from thanking guests for attending. When you see Rufus could you please tell him that I would like to speak to him before the end of the evening? No matter how hoarse my voice becomes I must congratulate him on his recent promotion."

Pollio Atticus grinned and briefly nodded his head at the centurion, before waving to another guest and walking over to shake his hand.

"Your father certainly knows how to put on a party," Maximus remarked, as another legion of slaves ushered past him, carrying trays of oysters, sliced melon, buttered asparagus, cured meats, spiced goose liver and various other foodstuffs that the soldier didn't even recognise.

"My father likes to project power, although given the choice of some of his decorations – and guests – I rather think he is sending out the message that money can't buy taste," Claudia replied, with an amused and askance expression, lingering a little on the sight of a woman with gold baubles in her hair like eggs in a bird's nest.

"You are your brother's sister Claudia." Maximus thought how Rufus would have said something similar, with a similar look on his face.

"Usually people say that I am my father's daughter."

"No. You're funnier and kinder than your father," Maximus replied, in earnest, with a meaningful look on his face.

"Unfortunately that's not too difficult." Claudia inwardly – and outwardly – beamed at the soldier's comment. She recalled the first time she had met him, at a lunch. At the beginning she had been bored, or rather had looked unimpressed to affect a sense of boredom, but she had soon warmed to the good humoured praetorian who her brother had spoken so highly of. Every time she had seen him subsequently she had been tinged with a little frustration and sadness that he was (happily) married. But she had still enjoyed his company. They were friends. And how many people could she say that about?

"True. You'll have to forgive me. It's been some time since I've had the opportunity to compliment a woman. I'm out of practise."

A collected gasp sounded out towards the other end of the garden, where the juggler had set fire to the daggers he was throwing, but Maximus and Claudia ignored the sound and spectacle.

"Well just to let you know I would be willing to let you practise on me some more, at any point. Flattery might get you everywhere with a woman."

Maximus laughed and Claudia thought how attractive the soldier was. There was a nobility, as well as ruggedness, to his features. There was a glow about him this evening too. Maybe it was due to him being home again, away from the frontier. Maybe it was due to the wine. Or maybe it was due to her. She sensed he might genuinely like her – and not just for her name, looks or the fact that she was the sister of his best friend. She beamed, brighter. She put her father's instructions out of her mind. She was with Maximus because she wanted to be with him.

"I'm sure you're not short of men complimenting you Claudia."

I am of real men – and real compliments.

"Well do not think that I am just idly complimenting you Gaius, but I'm glad to see you again. You're funnier and kinder than any other man present – although unfortunately that's not too difficult. Julia was fortunate to have you though. I never really knew you that well when she passed away – and I didn't really offer my condolences at the time. But you were in my thoughts. Did I ever tell you that I spent the afternoon with her once? We bumped into each other at the market and had lunch."

She was funnier and kinder than me. It's probably why he loved her so much.

"Julia mentioned it in a letter she sent me while I was serving in Egypt. She said that you made her laugh – and blush." Maximus recalled how his wife had also mentioned that Claudia seemed to be forever playing a part for others, whether she was dealing with her husband, father or other women. Yet behind the act there was a far more interesting and virtuous character trying to get out. "I felt that I was the more fortunate one between us though."

I still miss her.

"She was genuinely lovely. I liked her, although I also envied her a little for having married the only man in Rome that my brother could ever approve of, in terms of me marrying someone." Claudia's eyes flashed with warmth – and something else. "I'm not so sure my father would have approved of me marrying you, however."

"I'll take that as a compliment," Maximus replied, with warmth – and something else – in his tone too.

*

A couple of women, their faces pinched in disgust, walked away at the unseemliness of the barbaric and strange scene. Most remained wide-eyed and rooted to the spot, however, as the Chinaman took off his shirt and unsheathed his long, slightly curved sword. Pollio Atticus had instructed his bodyguard to give an exhibition of his skills, to entertain the guests at the party. His skin stretched over his face, like a reptile's. His body, marked by a number of gruesome scars, looked supple and muscular. A couple of the spectators gasped at the sight of the beastly looking foreigner.

Chen proceeded to run through a display of lightning quick and unorthodox sword drills, shouting out in his native language to add a further air of colour and ferocity. Large melons were placed on tripods, which his razor sharp blade sliced in two, without knocking them over. The Chinaman remained stone-faced, apart from his lip curling up slightly in contempt for the ignoble people who made up his audience, but he soon began to inwardly enjoy the attention of some of the women who applauded him.

"He's very skilled, isn't he?" a lissom teenage girl giddily proclaimed, whilst clutching the arm of an indifferent looking centurion.

"Yes. It must have taken him years to learn how to defeat a melon, or cut thin air in two," Rufus Atticus replied (loud enough for the Chinaman to hear) to the over-excited Lucilla.

52

As much as his father always encouraged Atticus to join the Senate when he spoke to him, his mother was constantly trying to get her son to marry. Although both institutions shared the same skill sets of lying and spending other peoples' money the soldier wasn't ready to commit to either quite yet. His mother persisted, however, and, after catching up with her son, she had introduced him to Lucilla, the youngest daughter of a frontrunner for a consulship. The constant jangling from the various items of jewellery Lucilla wore (bangles, anklets, necklaces) nearly annoyed Atticus as much as the sound of her shrill voice. Her teeth were too large and her brain was too small, he judged.

She's more horse than woman.

Lucilla giggled, or rather whinnied, at the handsome officer's comment, having nervously laughed at every other joke Atticus had made since being introduced to him (he had just commented how he would rather swallow his sword than any further verses from the poet in residence at the party). The sound of her squealing laughter, as well as the praetorian's sarcastic comment, disturbed Chen's concentration and he knocked over the tripod when slicing the final melon in two. Atticus let out a burst of goading laughter, witnessing the Chinaman's mistake.

"We've had a juggler, now it seems my father has offered us up a clown for our amusement," the soldier loudly remarked whilst applauding, causing the audience around him to laugh with him.

The assassin's narrow eyes widened in rage. He snorted and glowered at the arrogant young officer. Chen tightly gripped the handle of his sword and his knuckles turned white as he envisioned slicing the praetorian's head off like a melon. Yet his antagonist was his master's son. The Chinaman believed the man to be disloyal and dishonourable. Rufus Atticus had helped to thwart his father's plans three years ago, when he had aided the German boy and his sister to reach the northern frontier. The soldier also served the Emperor, their enemy. But his master had given the assassin express orders to spare his son's life.

"I wish to first find out the reason why my son has come back to Rome. Dead men can't talk. Also, dead men can't fuck. I need my son to produce an heir. Claudia may well be barren... Rufus provides my best hope to carry on our name and bloodline... The needs of the family must even prove sovereign over my desire for revenge..."

Atticus continued to wear an amused expression on his face as his father's bodyguard continued to glare at him as if he wanted to kill him. Atticus remembered how one of the Emperor's agents had reported that a Chinaman had been responsible for the distribution of negative propaganda. The praetorian had thought of his father's bodyguard when reading the document – and had grown suspicious.

"Chen, isn't it? That was a fine display. You must be of great use to my father, especially when he is in need of a fruit salad. Or do you have any other talents?" Atticus was keen to provoke his father's bodyguard, to either help ruin the party or substantiate his suspicions.

The assassin walked towards the soldier with fire in his eyes, muscles rippling along his sweat-glazed arms.

"I have other talents too. You may even get to see them soon, close up. You may not be so willing to mock me then," Chen threatened, almost in a whisper. His hand wrapped itself around the ivory handle of his sword.

"Oh I'm not so sure about that. The more I get to know someone the more I usually find reason to mock them. It seems you want to teach me a lesson though Chen. Did you hire the brigand Bulla to try and teach me a lesson all those years ago too?"

The simmering Chinaman's blood was about to boil over. He was about to confess his crime and answer yes. He would prove to the impudent Roman that he didn't need to hire Bulla or anyone else to teach him a lesson. He was superior to the white man in every way, indeed the Chinaman considered the Roman to be the barbarian out the two of them. He belonged to the master race.

"Master Rufus, sorry to disturb you but your father wishes to see you in the house. If you would like to accompany me," Sextus, one of Pollio Atticus' attendants, remarked. Sextus had served in the household for over a decade. The all-seeing Pollio had observed his bodyguard approach his son. The statesman quickly instructed his slave to part the two men, for fear of Chen doing or saying something out of turn.

The centurion sighed but agreed to see his father – and not just because he wanted to free himself from the cloying Lucilla.

*

Rufus Atticus sat in the triclinium, waiting for his father. He noticed how the marble floor had been retiled, again. Every five years the house was redecorated. Projecting wealth was as good as projecting power. The most expensive, as opposed to the best, works of art hung on the walls. It wasn't just the unfamiliar decor which made Atticus feel like he was a stranger in a strange house though. The palatial property always felt more akin to a mausoleum than a home, a museum dedicated to affluence and the history of his family. The library – and tavern – had felt more like home to him when he had been a teenager.

The soldier looked out onto the party. All of his father's cronies were present. He saw Senator Antonius Reburrus, snaking his arm around the Chinese wife of a wealthy silk merchant. His tan was as well-oiled as his hair. Antonius, a former consul, had manipulated the senate five years ago into invading a region in Persia, rich in natural resources. He now served as a special peace envoy to a neighbouring province in the area. Such had been his increase in wealth since he left office that no one could accurately judge the extent of his fortune. Atticus had also noticed Antonius' wife, Sabina, at the party earlier. She was equally self-serving and rapacious as her husband, if not more so. Sabina came from a family of distinguished advocates. It was perhaps no coincidence that during Antonius' consulship the number of laws which came onto the statute books had increased threefold compared to the previous year. As Atticus had once heard Sabina's father exclaim, "It's simple. The more laws we have the more money we can make." Sabina had been so concerned with making money over the past few years though that the glare of gold had blinded her to her husband's frequent affairs. And what did Antonius and his wife do with their wealth? Buy even more modish, vulgar works of art than his father and spend money as if he were a consul still, or an Emperor. No matter how many expensive outfits Sabina bought, however, she would still be mutton dressed up as mutton, Atticus mused.

A guttural, wine-fuelled laugh drew the centurion's attention to Julius Porticus. His chin, or rather chins, swayed as he laughed. He was just about to tell a fellow guest how much of "a man of the people" he was, having once served as the head of a carpenter's gild. The former praetor was still under investigation for defrauding the treasury. Not only had he been accused of embezzling funds, which had been set aside in the budget for the maintenance of the city's aqueducts, but Porticus had also used public money to buy a house on the Palatine Hill. His argument was that if he lived and worked out of his villa, situated just outside the capital, then he wouldn't have been able to do his job to the best of his abilities. The tragedy was, Atticus thought, that Porticus *had* done his job to the best of his abilities. The aqueducts still needed repairing and the official inquiry into his crimes had gone on for so long that most people had forgotten about it. He was helped by being able to employ his uncle, Sabina's father, as his advocate. He also attended the same school as Antonius and was friends with a number of senators who had been asked to form the committee to oversee his case.

The sneer on Atticus' face betrayed the sneer in his thoughts as he saw Gnaeus Varro standing next to Porticus. Varro had spent the first two years of the war against the Marcomanni campaigning to reduce the rations and men that the Empire devoted to servicing the legions. For the past two years, however, after inheriting an estate which included property situated on the frontier and a foundry in Ravenna which manufactured arms, Varro had tirelessly petitioned the Senate to furnish the Emperor with more men and equipment. His slogan now was, "Let's finish the job." Suffice to say Varro was in the process of selling a number of shares in the foundry to his senatorial colleagues, in order to win the argument and give Marcus Aurelius "the tools to finish what the enemy started."

Even Hercules would be at pains to clean Rome's augean stables, Atticus thought. Perhaps it was now only corruption and hypocrisy holding everything together. In the days of the Republic many of his father's guests would have been sewn up in a sack with a wild animal and thrown into the Tiber for their crimes. Perhaps a greater punishment would be to throw them all into a sack and make them suffer each other's conversation for an eternity.

"Rufus, thank you for waiting and for meeting me," Pollio Atticus amiably said, the iciness having melted from the tone of their previous encounter. Rufus remained seated and silent. He decided that he would allow his father to do most of the talking when they met, partly in hope that he would say too much. The statesman offered his son a conciliatory expression, which seemed genuine.

"I want you to know that I haven't come back from the war to become embroiled in a different type of conflict," Rufus exclaimed, wary of his father but still willing to hear him out.

"I know. And I understand. It's unusual for me to apologise, as either a politician or father, but I want to say I'm sorry Rufus. I was wrong. I was wrong for trying to prevent you from joining the army. And I was wrong to doubt that you would succeed. I know you think that I do not have a high opinion of the Emperor, but we have shared a number of letters these past few years. He has been kind enough to apprise me of your wellbeing and advancement. And I understand congratulations are in order, in regards to your promotion... As a politician and father you have been a victim of listening to a countless number of my speeches, but please now hear me out. The Empire is divided enough for a father to be in dispute with his only son. I am asking you to forgive my pride – and stupidity... I will no longer ask you to give up your career in the army for a career in politics. You are your own man. And if the Emperor is happy having you fight by his side, who am I to argue with him? Yet I would like you to consider taking a wife Rufus. Before I would have argued that you should be doing this for yourself, or that it would make your mother happy to see you married. But you know me better than that. I am asking for selfish reasons."

"Master, sorry to disturb you," Sextus remarked, entering the room and interrupting the senator. "But it is a matter of some importance."

"No, Sextus. *This* is a matter of some importance, talking to my son. Unless Nero is burning down Rome again any other business can wait," the statesman said firmly, but not too harshly, to his attendant.

Sextus gave a brief nod of his head and retreated.

"Now, where was I?"

"I was about to get my new wife pregnant," Rufus said.

"I'm not asking you to give me a decision here and now. I would just like you to think about things. The old Pollio Atticus, as you know, would have demanded to select your wife for you. But I trust you will marry wisely. We both want you to be happy. I will also instruct your mother not to interfere either, as much as she may choose to burn down Rome at hearing such news... Do you know how long you will be back with us for? Has the Emperor said anything to you about why he has returned to the capital and when he is planning to return to the north? It's just that it would be nice to arrange a family dinner while you are here... I now realise, Rufus, that for far too long I devoted myself to becoming the father of my country, as opposed being the father of my children."

"I'm unsure how long I will be in the capital for. The Emperor is due to make an important announcement soon. I'm unable to say any more on the matter though. I hope you understand. I will also consider what you have just said. I've changed, I think. Maybe I am ready to marry. Of course that could just be the wine talking."

Pollio Atticus grinned at his son's jest and warmly clasped him on the shoulder.

"I understand, in regards to your need to be discreet and I also understand how you have changed. I hope to prove to you how much I have changed too."

Aye, but a snake which sheds its skin is still a snake.

11.

Marcus Aurelius stood up and walked around his desk in order to bid a farewell to Gaius Avidius Cassius, after their meeting together discussing the politics and strategy in the east.

Cassius cut an imposing figure and physically dwarfed Aurelius. Broad shouldered and strong jawed, a pair of dark, doubtless eyes hung over an aquiline nose. The military commander smiled, or rather smirked, as he firmly clasped the hand of the man he was cuckolding. Avidius Cassius was a descendant of the Seleucid King Antiochus IV – and some senators remarked that he was beginning to rule over the peoples in the east as if he were a monarch. He was a disciplinarian – in regards to both his own soldiers and also the civilian population – whose ambition and pride often clouded his judgement. His authoritarian behaviour was not the solution to the problem of increasing rebellion in the east, but rather the cause of it, some considered. Others argued that ruthless commanders such as Cassius were a necessary evil for running the Empire.

Cassius had cause to believe in himself, even if others didn't. The commander had been instrumental in winning a series of brilliant victories during the Parthian War, although the co-Emperor at the time, Lucius Verus, was unfairly given the credit for his triumphs. Marcus Aurelius had recognised the soldier's abilities, however, and proceeded to promote him, to the point where Cassius now held imperium over a number of provinces and legions in the east. Cassius had shown loyalty and gratitude towards his Emperor during the early part of his career, but he now believed he was worthy enough to usurp his place on the throne – as well as his place in his wife's bed. He recalled Pollio Atticus' remark, that he had more royal blood running through his veins than the Emperor. He had promised Pollio that if and when the time came he would do his duty and succeed Aurelius, "for Rome's sake." Cassius would concede that the Emperor had brought stability (and he thanked the Gods that Aurelius rather than the debauchee Lucius Verus had become sole Emperor) but stability wasn't progress. Cassius believed that he could win the war in the north, even if he had to burn down every tree that a barbarian could hide behind.

I am younger and stronger than him... and my bloodline is nobler. He is old, tired... I'm not even sure how much he still wishes to be Emperor.

Faustina had confessed to Cassius how Aurelius had sex with his wife out of duty, rather than desire.

One should enjoy, rather than just endure, being a Caesar... Pollio Atticus is right. It isn't just the plague weakening the Empire, it is the Emperor...

The soldier continued to smile and shake the Emperor's hand. Aurelius thanked the commander for meeting with him and for giving up his evening. Cassius sniggered to himself, however, thinking of the amount of late nights he had spent in the Imperial Palace attending to the Empress. Aurelius finally asked after his friend's family and wished them well, before the two men parted.

The Emperor sat in, or rather slumped into, his chair. He sighed – and nearly blew out a candle as he did so. The oak chair creaked as his bones cracked. He barely noticed, or cared, as one of the oil lamps in the chamber went out. Two different tonics, in purple ceramic phials, stood on his desk. Both were from Galen. One was concocted to help the

Emperor sleep, the other to keep him awake so he could work through the night.

Cassius is a good soldier, but I'm not so sure that he is a good man.

Marcus Aurelius could not help but compare his commander in the east with Gaius Maximus. The Emperor recalled the quote from Juvenal, after re-reading the satirist yesterday afternoon; he thought about how apt the words were to describe the officer.

Many individuals have, like uncut diamonds, shining qualities beneath a rough exterior.

Marcus Aurelius reflected that Cassius' breastplate was polished but his soul was besmirched – as much as Faustina spoke well of his character. The Emperor once again sighed – and then reached for one of the phials.

12.

Aurelia began to doubt whether the body was wholly separate from the soul as both thrummed with happiness while she lay next to Maximus. She'd finally caught her breath back. Aurelia placed her palm on his chest and her racing heart slowed, attuning itself to the calm, contented, beat of his.

The morning after the party Maximus had visited Galen at his house, but then in the afternoon he had come to see Aurelia. They had had lunch in the garden and had spoken about their future.

"I don't want to wait any longer," Aurelia had said, sunlight gilding her soft features. Desire had (just about) overcome her nervousness. She wanted to be with Maximus. She had thought about little else the sleepless evening and morning before. Maximus had cradled her face in his hands and kissed her – before taking her hand and leading her up to the bedroom. She had felt awkward, passive, at first. Maximus had been gentle, as well as passionate. Something soon awoke in the woman though – a fire was lit – and Aurelia had given herself to him, body and soul. It was like nothing she had ever felt before. She had gasped and sighed. She had closed her eyes, arched her back in pleasure and while many Christians might have deemed that she was living in sin, Aurelia had suddenly felt like she was in heaven.

Helena had nearly dropped the plate she was cleaning as she heard the floorboards – and her mistress – groan.

Aurelia now rested her head upon Maximus' chest, after making love for the third time. Motes of dust sparkled from the amber sunlight pouring through the window. Maximus breathed in her perfume and lovingly put his arm around her, his fingertips caressing her silken, tingling skin. He wanted as much of their bodies to touch as possible. Maximus hadn't been with another woman since his wife had passed away, although before Julia he had slept with any number of serving girls, whores, and women bored with their husbands.

"Thank you for waiting for me Gaius... Thank you for saving my life three years ago – and for saving me from a half-lived life now."

"You were worth the wait," Maximus replied, smiling as he recalled Galen's comment from earlier. "Aurelia needs a man in her life, other than Jesus Christ."

"I want to get married... I don't want to replace Julia though. I'm me... But I don't want you to think that I want you to forget about her. She's part of you."

Maximus had vigorously shaken his head as he had sat beside his wife on her deathbed, when Julia had said that he should find another wife after she was gone. The soldier had shaken his head to convey that he wouldn't, or couldn't, love again. And because his wife shouldn't say such things – because he had believed she was going to live. Julia was still with him, through his memories and dreams. For a couple of months or so during the past three years Maximus had stopped writing to Aurelia, believing that he was somehow being unfaithful to Julia by having feelings for someone else. But Julia would have wanted him to be happy. He needed something in his life, besides death and duty. And so the centurion had commenced to write to Aurelia again... Maximus no longer felt guilty in wanting to be with Aurelia. He would still cherish his time with Julia, but he was ready to love and marry again.

The praetorian did feel guilty, however, in that, after leaving Aurelia's bed, he would be spending the evening with Claudia.

13.

The four men had just finished their shift on guard duty at Pollio Atticus' house. They squatted down in the courtyard under a sweltering sky and drew out a large circle in chalk. One of the men, Titus, a former lictor, retrieved his jar containing a number of large beetles. Each man proceeded to pick and mark an insect on its back. Money and banter were exchanged. A jug of sour wine was also passed around. The beetles were placed in the centre of the ring and the race commenced for the first one to cross the line of the circle. The men cheered their champions on as if the black bugs were charioteers in the arena. More bets were placed. One man started to plan what he would spend his winnings on as his beetle energetically scurried towards the chalk line – before energetically changing direction to head back to the centre of the circle. He swore enough to make a lady, or harlot, blush.

The cheers and excitement increased, nearly reaching a crescendo, as two of the insects neared the finishing line together. Titus, who had called his beetle "Fury", started to call out his name in order to spur it on to victory. Just as the insect was about to get chalk on its legs, as well as its back, a large boot squashed "Fury" in its moment of glory, as Chen callously ruined the men's sport and the atmosphere. The Chinaman grunted as he strode on towards the house, to meet with his master. Titus cursed the yellow-skinned barbarian beneath his breath, rather than out loud.

He's a dog… But every dog has its day.

Chen sneered-cum-smirked as he pictured the shocked and resentful expressions behind his back. The Chinaman considered the puny guards to be mere insects themselves –

and their hatred of him fed his sense of amusement and power. He spared the guards little more thought, though, as he continued to walk towards the house where he was due to report to Atticus in his study. Chen's sneer turned into a fully-fledged smirk as he thought of how he would ask permission to possess his master's daughter again as a reward once the mission was complete.

*

I must be Caesar, rather than Catiline… I cannot risk everything – and fail.

Pollio Atticus stood in front of three drawings on the wall. One was a map of the whole of Rome, another focused on the area around the grain warehouse on the river and the final one was a plan of the warehouse itself. He noticed his fingers were stained with ink from composing more propaganda. Soon he would have blood on his hands. But he was doing what he was doing for Rome.

The ends justify the means... Tomorrow night will be the beginning of the end... You may be stoical enough in the face of impending starvation Aurelius, but the mob won't be… The first thing I'll do when you're gone is pay the army a donative, their full purses will fill the void of your absence… The people too can be bought off, as easily as a politician. Virgil wrote that "Fickle and changeable always is women." The line may be applied to the mob too…

Chen stood attentive to his master as a determined Pollio Atticus ran through the plan again. The agent would lead his main force, carrying arms and barrels of highly flammable oil, up the street which ran alongside the river towards the grain warehouse. They would easily best the small number of men guarding the warehouse. Once inside his men would douse the grain in the oil and set fire to the food supplies. A number of men also needed to be designated to cover the outside of the warehouse – and surrounding buildings – with graffiti, blaming the Emperor and the regime for being the cause of the desperate act. Pollio Atticus reiterated that it was important, however, that Chen did not let his men run riot. They should not set fire to any other buildings. They should not loot. When entering and exiting the city they should do so in small groups to avoid raising any suspicion. Although Chen's force would appear to be acting as an angry, desperate mob his men needed to conduct themselves with proficiency and professionalism.

The Praetorian Guard would be unable to muster a sufficient enough force in time to stop Chen's men, but if any opposition did arrive on the scene then he should deal with the enemy accordingly. *Dead men tell no tales*.

"You can enjoy yourself," Pollio Atticus said to the warrior, who would relish testing himself against the best that Rome had to offer in the form of the Emperor's elite soldiers.

Chen thought he would particularly enjoy himself if somehow Maximus or his master's son were on duty and ordered to deal with the disturbance. The agent felt he had unfinished business with the pair after failing in his mission three years ago. He would also be happy to provide Rufus Atticus with another close-up display of his abilities. Since their encounter at the party the assassin had imagined killing the centurion in more ways than one.

Pollio Atticus afforded himself a smile as he finally explained how he would provide men to help put out the fire later in the evening. The statesman also enjoyed the irony that the Emperor would soon be betrayed by one of his most loyal officers. Gaius Maximus had accepted his daughter's invitation to dinner.

His secrets will soon be hers – and mine.

14.

A bulbous moon swelled, ripe, in the night sky. The shutters were opened throughout the house to let in a cooling breeze and freshen up the oppressive, muggy air.

Desire – and something even nicer – fluttered inside Claudia as she prepared herself for her evening with Maximus. She remembered, from a conversation many years ago, what he liked to eat and asked her cook to produce a number of dishes accordingly. She wanted him to have what he wanted, rather than what she thought would impress him.

At first she tried on the outfit that she thought her father would have wanted her to wear – a low-cut stola, without her strophium, made from translucent red silk. A long, unsubtle slit ran up the sides of the garment – showing off her tawny legs. The cut of the stola hugged her figure, to the point of constricting her... But the outfit had looked, or felt, wrong.

Instead Claudia chose her favourite summer dress and she saw, for once, a smiling face staring back at her as she looked into the polished silver mirror. Her dresser thought, for once, that her mistress appeared happy – and all the prettier for it. She had a glow about her. Her hairdresser was given the evening off as Claudia decided to wear her long hair down, how she liked it and how Julia used to wear it. Usually her hairdresser had to pin the lady's hair up and construct an edifice worthy of Archimedes. Claudia also, for a change, barely wore any make-up. She reddened not her lips with ochre, to make them appear fuller, nor thickened her eyebrows with soot. To finish off her outfit Claudia asked her dresser to fetch her gold and sapphire brooch, in the shape of a swan, which her grandmother had given to her when she was barely a teenager. As her dresser fastened the brooch on her left breast Claudia recalled the speech that the formidable – and funny – aristocratic woman had given to her, when she had first pinned the heirloom on her.

"You'll soon learn, my girl, that it isn't all that easy being a woman of your class in Rome. You have to play dumb more than an actress and smile more than a politician does around election time… And it only gets a little easier the older – and the more practised – you get. As much as you may change, unfortunately men and society won't… Just wake up every day and try to do more good than ill. And grow old gracefully, or disgracefully, depending on your mood… Try to marry a good, as well as a rich, man – and if he's neither then attempt to turn him into both… Failing that, take a lover who can put a smile on your face and money in your purse."

*

The breeze whispered into the murmuring braziers. Claudia had arranged for them to eat in the moonlit garden. The scent of summer flowers proved welcome to Maximus, after having breathed in certain other aromas over the past week that Rome had to offer, but the smell of grilled fish and meat was heavenly for the soldier.

He had been served with oysters for a first course and lobster claws for his second, but Maximus' eyes truly widened in satisfaction when he came eye to eye with the honey-glazed suckling pig. If the soldier had been in the presence of his men, rather than that of a lady, he might have even salivated. It made her happy to see him so happy. The look of surprise – and pleasure – on his face was akin to that of when he had seen her for the first time that evening, Claudia thought. He had never looked at her in such a revealing – and amorous – way before. Perhaps he had always thought of her as his friend's sister. Maybe it was because he had been happily married before, or he had thought her happily married. For a moment Maximus had been speechless, captivated. His heart had been in his mouth when she walked down the stairs to greet him. Before long though they had started to talk and laugh like old friends. Maximus revealed how the Emperor had asked him to remain in Rome, rather than return north with him. Claudia calmly replied that he might now get bored serving on guard duty, compared to the dangers of the frontier, but her heart sang at the news that the officer would be staying in the capital.

Oil lamps hung above them under an awning and shone upon her burnished skin. The light caught her brooch and silver earrings – and winked at him like the stars. Maximus drained his cup of wine again and openly admired his seductive host. He seemed equally as intoxicated by the wine as he was by her beauty.

In another world, in another life, I could and should be with her.

Father wants me to be Calypso. Perhaps I've played that part for so long I'm unable to be anyone else. But I want to be, for once, Penelope – faithful, loved and worth coming home to… I want him to see my goodness, rather than guile.

"So how did Rufus react to the news that you were having dinner with me this evening?" Claudia asked, with the hint of a smile on her face from picturing the shock on her brother's usually relaxed features.

"I'll let you know once I tell him. He may well be more upset with me for not sharing this suckling pig with him, than sharing the news that I had dinner with his sister."

"I'm sure that Rufus will forgive you on both counts. He's very fond of you Gaius, and my brother isn't fond of many people as you know, aside from other men's wives. But I'm very fond of you too. I want you to know that I didn't just invite you to dinner because you are my brother's best friend. You mean more to me than that."

They shared a meaningful look, for a moment.

"It's also not just because I need a lady to practise my compliments on that I accepted your invitation Claudia. My compliments to your cook too, by the way."

Maximus gulped down another half-cup of fine wine. He drank to forget himself, or rather to forget about Aurelia. Yet he remembered her words – and the contentedness in her expression – when he had parted from her that afternoon.

"I'll let you say goodbye now. But when you come back you'll be coming back to me for the rest of your life," she had said as he parted.

Maximus willed himself to concentrate on the woman in front of him, rather than the woman inside his head and heart.

"Well it's partly because you never showered me with cliché-ridden compliments that I noticed you all those years ago Gaius. Most men used to put me on a pedestal only so that they could look up my skirt, I'm afraid. But you were, or are, different. You're the most honourable man I know. You've always been nice to me, even when I haven't always deserved such treatment."

They shared another meaningful look, for a longer, lasting, moment. Neither knew who held the other's hand across the table first.

"I wish we could have somehow done this in the past Claudia. Have dinner. Spend the evening together. Talk. I had the right feelings, but it was never the right time. But it's the right time now."

Night time. Bedtime.

*

"Morning," Claudia purred. Her slender legs were coiled around Maximus'. A fragrant film of massage oil still glazed

72

Claudia's body and shone in the honey-tinged sunlight. His head throbbed.

The night before hadn't felt like the first time for Claudia, but it had felt like the best time. She had first asked Maximus – but then almost ordered the soldier later in the night – to make love to her. She had wanted him inside her, so much for so long. She squeezed his hand as the pleasure increased, as he kissed her lips, thighs, breasts and... She wanted him to love her like Odysseus loved Penelope.

"Morning," Maximus replied. He felt fatigued, as though he had just spent the night in battle. Yet the centurion found the strength to kiss, deliciously, the remarkable woman again. His fingertips caressed and ran down her back, buttocks and legs. She hummed in satisfaction, breakfasting on the sensation.

"Hmmm, I could get used to waking up to you like this," Claudia smilingly remarked, hungrily kissing him on the chest and then on the mouth in reply, her hands swirling around his body beneath the silk sheets.

"I could too. I'm not so sure your husband could though."

"Fronto is a joke, which I have to suffer the punch line to. We live separate lives already. He means nothing to me. We'd commit to divorcing each other with more passion to that of what we had when we married each other... I feel like my whole life has been plotted out for me by my father, social convention and by the role I must play as an aristocratic woman and wife. I want for nothing, materially. On the outside my life may seem like a comedy, with the happiest of happy endings. But being adored is not the same as being loved. A palace can still be a prison. I want someone I can grow old, not bored, with."

My life is a tragedy. Yet you can write another act into it. Be the hero.

Maximus felt more sympathy, than love, for the woman but hoped his expression wasn't betraying mere pity.

"I'm not sure that I'll be able to keep pace with you."

"I'll wait for you – and if I fall behind, wait for me. Spend the day with me Gaius."

"Unfortunately I have to spend the day with the Emperor, as much as I'd rather attend to a goddess than a god. But Aurelius is due to deliver some important – and good – news soon. I need to ask you to keep this to yourself, but we may be about to defeat a greater enemy than boredom even – that of the plague. Galen believes that he has identified a cure. He has still to run some final tests at the laboratory at his house, but it seems that more people will now get the opportunity to grow old together."

"That's wonderful news," Claudia enthused, but her happiness was as much for her finding love as for Galen finding a cure. They embraced and kissed each other – and she didn't want to let him go. "We should celebrate, tonight."

Maximus agreed, sorrowfully thinking how he had also agreed to spend the evening with Aurelia. He was breaking his word – and his heart.

15.

Duty called. Shortly after Maximus left at midday to return to his barracks – and then see the Emperor – Claudia went to report to her father. A slither of her soul was tempted to keep her word to Maximus and keep the news of Galen's cure a secret. Yet the fear of her father finding out that she had kept intelligence from him shaped her thoughts – and she ordered her litter bearers to wend their way through Rome's busy streets even faster than usual. Her husband – and the law – could provide little protection should she earn her father's displeasure by betraying him (or "the family," as he would argue). Claudia had witnessed her father ruin the lives and reputations of his enemies many times before, indeed she had occasionally been involved in the process.

Chen led the slightly agitated and slightly perspiring woman through the house towards Pollio Atticus' study. Despite the sultry summer heat Claudia still felt a chill run down her spine in the Chinaman's presence. She shivered as she felt his lecherous eyes crawl over her. Every so often her father would order his daughter to spend the night with the Chinaman, as a reward for his agent's work and loyalty.

Pollio Atticus appeared pensive at best, saturnine at worst, when Claudia entered his study. The shutters were closed, yet still a little sunlight bled through. He looked at her both sternly and expectantly. His brow was as creased as the silk sheets on her bed, she thought fleetingly. Atticus had covered over two of the three maps on his wall (leaving only the general map of the city visible) out of precaution. Claudia, however, was already aware of her father's scheme to cause unrest by destroying the capital's grain supply. Some months ago, during the last time her father had rewarded his bodyguard, Chen had sought to impress Claudia by revealing how he had become her father's most trusted agent – and he spoke of their grand plans. Pillow talk.

"Did he talk?" the statesman asked, with little concern for the wellbeing of his daughter.

"They always talk. It seems that the Emperor has returned to Rome to make the announcement that he, or rather Galen, has found a cure for the plague. The doctor is currently running some final tests at his house, but Maximus is meeting with Aurelius today. The Emperor will make his proclamation soon, maybe even in a day or two."

Pollio Atticus remained impassive at hearing his daughter's brief report. Yet he subtly exhaled, flaring his nostrils – and he made a fist around the stylus he was holding. He cursed Aurelius – and Galen – beneath his breath. His blood coursed like lava around his body. The senator had had visions of late of the warehouse in flames, and now he felt like that his plans – dreams – could turn to ash. Should Aurelius prove responsible for delivering a cure to the plague – and saving the Empire – he would be hailed as a new Augustus. Any support that Atticus could currently count on in the Senate would drain away, like sand through his fingertips, should he or Avidius Cassius challenge Aurelius' authority. The Empire would be soon be feasting, rather than starving, at hearing the good news. Agriculture and the economy would thrive again. The army would serve its Emperor with even greater fervour. Aurelius saving the Empire would condemn Atticus to being no more than a footnote in history.

He must be stopped. There is still time.

Aurelius could only announce that he was in possession of a cure, if it was true. It appeared that the remedy only resided in

Galen's laboratory – and inside the scientist's head – at the present time. He could destroy both, tonight.

Desperate times call for desperate measures.

Chen still needed to command the mission at the warehouse. So he would personally lead a few men and pay a visit to the physician. He would need to interrogate Galen and assess the situation himself. He could make things look like a robbery and/or arson. He may need to abduct the doctor. He could leave the burnt corpse of a slave in the laboratory as a substitute for Galen. The secret of the cure would seemingly die with him. But when the time was right Pollio Atticus would make the announcement that he had discovered a remedy for the scourge – and be proclaimed the saviour of Rome. *Augustus. Caesar.*

No. All is not lost.

Claudia broke the silence as her father sat, slate-faced, deep in thought. She willed herself to bury her feelings for Maximus deep down inside her as she spoke about him.

"From what I could gather Maximus is close to the Emperor. I could continue to see him. He could prove a useful source of intelligence."

Atticus' hard eyes turned upon his daughter. He looked at first as if he were about to reprove her for speaking out of turn and disturbing his thoughts, but then he suddenly smiled.

"I agree. Yet sooner or later, or sooner rather than later, the irksome soldier will be sleeping underground rather than in your bed. He'll fall, along with Aurelius. Hopefully he won't need to put his oafish paws on you for much longer. Chen will take care of things, when the time comes. Won't you Chen?"

The Chinaman nodded and grinned. There was a glint in his eye, like sunlight shining off the polished blade of his sword.

Claudia's heart cracked, but her face remained unchanged. Pollio Atticus had taught his daughter how to mask her emotions many years ago, to such an extent that it had become second nature. Ecstasy was feigned during agony. The dusting of make-up that Claudia wore cracked not, either in a smile or frown, as she appeared indifferent to the fate of the centurion. But she was far from indifferent. Something had broken inside of her – and in doing so something else had slotted into place.

He must be stopped.

"Continue to extract what intelligence you can out of the praetorian. Find out about his meeting with Aurelius today. Well done though Claudia. I am pleased with you. See your mother's dressmaker on your way out. Treat yourself to a new outfit, on my account. Perhaps you may wish to arrange an outfit for Gaius Maximus' funeral. Something that you can wash the crocodile tears out from," the statesman drily remarked – and chuckled at his own joke.

Claudia smiled, serpent-like.

"I will order the dress."

But the funeral will be yours.

"Thank you. That will be all. Now please leave us."

As much as she wanted to be party to her father's intentions and plans Claudia dutifully obeyed the order. She remained in earshot, however, to hear her father remark, "We will still proceed as planned tonight. I have a special task for you beforehand though."

16.

Night time slowly but surely commenced to bleed into the horizon. The temperature dropped. The clinking of armour sounded over the cawing of the birds who circled over the barracks. A brawny centurion, who led a dozen of his men across the courtyard, barked out the order of "Eyes front" as an optio accompanied a finely dressed woman through the complex. Claudia did not notice the ogling looks, however, as she walked quickly, in order to meet with her brother. Her head was downcast – in thought, shame and worry.

He must be stopped.

Rufus Atticus stood up from behind his desk as his sister entered his small office. He looked at her neutrally, neither showing the surprise, anxiety nor pleasure which Claudia considered that he might, given that she had never visited him at the barracks before. Atticus did not say a word as she ran towards him and buried her head in his chest. The centurion soon felt tears on his shoulder.

"I've done something terrible. But I want to prevent something worse happening," Claudia confessed, her tears cutting scars through her make-up.

"I think that you had better sit down. Would you like some water, or wine, to help calm yourself?" Atticus remarked evenly, in stark contrast to his distressed sister.

"Water, please," the woman said quietly, struck by her brother's air of seriousness. She was used to him only being serious about his indifference – or enjoying himself. She briefly took in his desk, filled with correspondence and work.

Perhaps he has changed. Perhaps I have, or can, change too.

Rufus poured his sister a cup of water from the jug on the table. He then silently sat down and picked up his stylus, ready to make notes in regards to whatever Claudia was about to say – as if he would be interrogating her. Again Claudia was struck by her brother's cold, rather than concerned, demeanour. She also noted his lack of shock or curiosity at seeing her turn up at his barracks without notice. It was as if he had been expecting her.

"You mentioned the other afternoon, Rufus, how you hoped that I would someday surprise myself. I am going to surprise you also by what I have to say. Father asked me to seduce Gaius Maximus, in order to extract information out of him about the Emperor's intentions and his reasons for returning to the capital. I know that you are aware of how father has asked me to seduce other men in the past. In being a good daughter I have been a bad wife and person. You never judged me though in the past Rufus. Please do not judge me now as well, at least until I finish what I have to say. I do not want to lose you, as well as everything else. If you have thought ill of some of the immoral things I've done, know that I have loathed myself more. But when father ordered me to get close to Gaius I did so willingly. I have always liked him. I've also surprised myself by the realisation that I think I might love him. We spent last night together."

Claudia let her confession hang in the air. A silence passed between the brother and sister. In the background they could hear the sound of clanging swords and cheering as soldiers wagered on a fencing bout. The centurion seemed unperturbed by his sister's revelation, however, indeed there was even a hint of a knowing smile on his face.

"I am going to surprise you by what I have to say Claudia. The plan was not for you to seduce Gaius, but rather for Gaius to seduce you. Father may be powerful, but he's also predictable. I knew he would use you, like he's used you in the past. I'm just sorry that I have used you as well. We've suspected him of being an enemy of the state for some time. We just needed some proof. For once you were the victim of a honey trap. Have you passed on to father the information about Galen finding a cure to the plague? Have you baited the hook?"

A dozen thoughts galloped around the stunned woman's mind, kicking up dust. All was, momentarily, a blur. Claudia felt like crying again, but she no longer would be able to embrace her brother. Her world was turned upside down. The huntress had become the prey. When, or if, she saw Maximus again she didn't know whether she would fall into his arms or slap him around the face. Perhaps she would do both. Her father had used her for years. But this was a new hurt, a new betrayal. Claudia merely nodded in reply, unable to look at her brother.

"Do you know what he is now planning to do? Is he going to attempt to kill Galen and steal the cure?" Atticus asked, raising his voice a little and losing his composure. The centurion leaned across the desk, his eyes burning with curiosity – and something else. Despite Claudia looking distraught the soldier still needed to question his sister. Duty called.

"Yes," Claudia murmured, her chin buried in her chest. She seemed in a stupor. Pale. Half dead.

"The more you can tell me, the better it will be for you. If you can help bring father to justice then I can petition the Emperor to grant you immunity from prosecution. I do not want you sharing father's fate," Atticus said in earnest – and also to encourage her to confess. "Do you know his plans in regards to Marcus Pollux? He's been paying the grain administrator a substantial sum of money over the past few months." Agents of the Emperor had provided intelligence that the administrator was operating outside of his remit. But Atticus had discovered Pollux's links to his father – from both searching through papers in his office and sleeping with his wife.

"Father has recently recruited a force of mercenaries. He's intending to burn down the warehouse on the river which stores the city's grain surplus. He believes that starvation will feed civil unrest – and lead to a revolution. Chen will lead the attack tonight. Father has been paying Pollux to purchase private stores of grain from the east."

"Tonight?!"

For the first time in their meeting shock and condemnation could be traced in Atticus' expression as he glared at his sister. The bronze stylus bent in his hand as the officer made a fist.

"What time tonight?" he hurriedly asked, standing over his sister.

"I don't know," Claudia replied, with shame and fear in her voice.

"How many men does he have?" Atticus demanded, glowering.

"I don't know."

"The only thing I know is that you've either helped save or damn the Empire, depending on what happens this evening." Atticus shook his head, in disappointment at his sister and from experiencing a sense of doubt over whether he could manage the situation.

"I'm sorry, I'm sorry," Claudia tearfully repeated.

"Apollo!" the centurion shouted, calling in the young legionary who was standing to attention outside his office. The soldier entered, struck by a rare desperation in Atticus' voice and bearing.

"Yes, Sir," Apollo said, partly distracted by the sight of the officer's tearful, but still beautiful, sister sitting on the chair before him. Half of her pinned-up hair hung untidily down her face. Her usually fine eyes were puffy.

"Immediately muster as many men as you can on the parade ground – officers, legionaries, archers, even raw recruits. I'll need a couple of trusted messengers too – one to be despatched to the Emperor, another to Maximus."

Cassius Bursus nodded and departed.

"There is one more important thing Rufus. It's why I'm here. Father has instructed Chen to murder Gaius. He will do so after tonight."

"Then the bastard won't see the dawn," the centurion replied determinedly, as he pulled his sword belt around his waist.

He must be stopped.

"I care about him, more than you know. Do you think he may have feelings for me?" Claudia said, looking up, wide-eyed, at her brother – almost pleading him to say "yes".

"No. I've lied to you enough over the past week. I have no wish to lie to you now. Gaius is in love with Aurelia. He's going to live with her – and ask her to marry him. You mustn't now come between them Claudia. If Aurelia finds out about what happened last night then I'll know that it came from you – and you will then lose me if you ruin Gaius' happiness. The gods know that he deserves some."

Claudia's heart cracked, again. Perhaps the gods also knew that she deserved to be unhappy, the woman thought to herself. Her life had been a series of sins, strung out like jewels upon a necklace. But she believed that last night could not have been all an act. It had been real for her. Yet she loved him enough to not stand in the way of his happiness.

He's too good for me…

"I understand. I don't want to hurt him. Can you give a message to him though?"

"Of course," Atticus answered, with an air of understanding – realising how much pain, as well as shame, his sister must be enduring.

"Tell him he's still the most honourable man I know," Claudia said with sincerity and sadness, feeling more than half dead.

17.

Silvery-grey clouds marbled the night sky. The murky waters of the Tiber slapped against the jetty. A chill wind blew off the river. Cassius Bursus was just about to board a barge, along with a dozen fellow archers, after receiving his orders from Atticus.

"This is either my Venus – or Vulture – throw of the dice Apollo," the officer quietly said to his friend, feeling the need to confide in someone in the absence of Maximus. Atticus' usually calm and confident countenance was flecked with distress. A fear of failure was eclipsing a desire to succeed. He expected his first command to be in the forests of Germany, not on the streets of Rome. The centurion had mustered as many men as he could, as quickly as he could, to lead an advance force and protect the warehouse. Most of the Praetorian Guard had been off duty or outside of the barracks when he had heard about his father's plans to destroy the capital's grain surplus. He had left instructions to form-up and send a relief force to secure the warehouse, but at present the newly promoted officer only commanded around a hundred men to ward off the imminent attack.

"You'll be fine. What was it Maximus once said? Don't give me a great general, give me a lucky one. And you're the luckiest man I've ever met, Sir."

"Thanks for the – I think – vote of confidence. Let's hope my luck lasts out until the morning. If you make your arrows count, though, Apollo I may not need to rely on good fortune."

The two men shook hands and Atticus went back to address his men. He forced himself to smile, to give off an air of confidence. Yet, inside, he was mired in anxiety. *The burden of command.* Atticus wryly thought back to when he had been a poet, rather than a soldier, and the only things that he had had to worry about were writer's block and a broken heart. Now he needed to worry about the lives of the men under him – and a city and empire perishing.

Atticus ordered a small portion of his men to keep watch over the two narrow streets which led towards the warehouse. He also posted men to guard the entrances to the grain supply. The bulk of his force, however, was assembled before him in two ranks, across the main street which ran parallel to the river. The centurion began to notice the air mist up in front of him from the soldiers' breath. A few had a gleam in their eyes, looking forward to tasting glory or blood. Most of the men, their faces pale in the moonlight, wore more wary expressions though. The numbers and nature of the enemy were still unknown. Some doubtless hoped that it would all just prove to be a false alarm – and the only thing they would have to do battle with tonight would be a jug of wine back at the barracks.

Atticus thought about the many times he had lined up in a shield wall before – instead of facing it as he now was. He read the legionaries' faces and sympathised with how young he must have seemed, compared to other commanding officers. Gaius Maximus' optio was little substitute for Gaius Maximus. His reputation for conquests in the bedroom would mean nothing on the battlefield.

My first command could prove my last.

*

Blood marked the Chinaman's tunic from the task he had completed that night before meeting up with his small army of mercenaries. They were a force to be reckoned with, he judged with pride. Chen wanted to prove to his master that he could be a trusted leader of men, as well as a loyal lone assassin. The new regime would need new commanders. He hoped that

Pollio Atticus would recognise what a feat of cunning and logistics it had been to smuggle all his soldiers, and their weapons, into the city. He had also smuggled several barrels of flammable oil through the city gates via a wine merchant.

The men congregated in a square, close by to the grain warehouse. Nigh on two hundred men, dressed in ordinary civilian clothes which were concealing an array of cudgels and short swords, stood waiting to be unleashed. Many wished to just get on with the task, as the sooner they got their money the sooner they could spend it. Some of the men licked their lips at the prospect of committing an act of violence and terrorism. Rome, or the army, had made their lives a misery at some point. They would now take their revenge on the capital.

A few onlookers who lived around the square took in the ominous scene behind half-closed shutters. Others completely shut out the sight and sounds of the suspicious mob, not wanting any trouble. Calling on a force of vigils, or the Praetorian Guard even, could well lead to violence rather than prevent it.

Chen gave one last debrief to his six lieutenants, who were each responsible for a section of his army. He was confident that every man knew his purpose. Fear, as well as financial reward, would generate success, the Chinaman concluded. He reminded his officers that there should be no witnesses left at the warehouse. *Dead men tell no tales*. He also reminded his lieutenants of the plan to disperse the men throughout different districts in the capital, after the deed was done. *Nothing should be left to chance*. Chen pictured the warehouse ablaze – and also the Imperial Palace being stormed, after months of the capital facing starvation. Perhaps his master would let him take his daughter as his wife, as well as reward him with a generalship, when the dust settled. The Chinaman grinned revealing a set of swollen gums and rotten teeth.

This command will be the first of many.

*

Silence and apprehension hung in the air, like the smell of a corpse. Spray from the river chilled the men's faces. Fear of the unknown chilled their hearts. Atticus was lost for words. He didn't know whether to tell a joke or warn his men of the seriousness of the situation. The newly promoted centurion thought that the usually laconic Maximus would have known what to say. A row of blank, or defeated, expressions stood before him – looking to him for direction and inspiration. Leadership.

I'm failing them… Losing them. And if I lose them I'll lose the battle…

Atticus – and his men – were finally distracted from their mordant thoughts by the sound of distant voices and the low rumbling of footsteps. The centurion's ears pricked up and he raised his head and turned, as alert as a hunting dog.

The officer drew his sword – and the legionaries duly did the same. The metallic, scraping noise felt familiar, even comforting, to the centurion. Atticus squinted, trying to gauge the numbers and nature of the enemy appearing from around the end of the main avenue along the river. Atticus also recognised the sound of wagons trundling over cobblestones. Blades momentarily glinted in the moonlight. The oncoming force slowed, but halted not, as the front ranks took in the row of soldiers.

We're outnumbered. But we won't be out-fought.

Some veterans might have advised the centurion to attack – to seize the moment and the momentum. Others would have advised caution – to retreat and wait for reinforcements. Despite the gelid air a bead of sweat formed on the young officer's temple and ran down his jaw. His heart pounded like an army, either advancing or being routed.

Two options… Attack or retreat.

The number of the enemy continued to grow. Hydra-headed. Atticus began to discern the build and features of the front ranks of his father's mercenary force. They were well-built, with battle-hardened faces. As with his dinner parties, Pollio Atticus had spared no expense, Rufus thought. They were all former soldiers or gladiators, disciplined yet vicious.

Attack or retreat… Death or honour.

Atticus turned to observe dozens of legionaries staring at him, awaiting an order – any order. Their expressions faded into the background, however, as the centurion pictured his father, smiling in triumph at his failure.

Attack or retreat… There is no other option.

But there was. Instead of his father looming large in his mind's eye Atticus pictured Maximus.

Sometimes it's not a question of attacking or retreating. Sometimes all you can do is just hold the line.

18.

"I worry that we may be spoiling the child. He's becoming too wilful and selfish," Marcus Aurelius remarked to his wife in their bedroom, furrowing his already wrinkled brow. He wrinkled his nose too, from the pungent smell of the jasmine and rose of his wife's perfume.

"And by 'we', I take it you mean me?" Faustina replied, arching her plucked eyebrows. She briefly stopped brushing her long, auburn hair to offer her husband both a questioning and accusing look. "An Empress should be beyond reproach, even from an Emperor," her mother had once told her. Even when looking haughty the Empress still appeared desirable. Age had not withered her. Childbirth had failed to ruin her figure. For once poets and fawning courtiers could be sincere when they complimented their Empress on her beauty. She had inherited her large, coquettish eyes from her mother – and could express attentiveness or boredom within the blink of an eye. All of her life Faustina had either been the daughter of an Emperor, or wife to one. She seldom believed she was playing a part, as she was seldom off stage. She was *Augusta*, far more even than her husband was an *Augustus*. He had been adopted, whereas she was noble.

As a young girl Faustina had loved her father dearly, and had taken instruction from her mother about being Empress. When duty called Faustina answered it. She had been married at fourteen, but quickly became at ease in the bedroom and at court. She had smiled when she needed to, praised the right gods on the right feast days, behaved with majesty or humility before the people depending on the occasion, could say

"Welcome" in over a dozen different languages and had provided the Empire with heirs.

Early on in her marriage the people had praised Faustina for her fecundity. Coinage was also minted, honouring the Emperor's wife for her chastity (Rufus Atticus had nicknamed it "funny money" at the time, aware as he was of the Empress' infidelities). Once Rome's favourite daughter in her youth, Faustina was now called the "Mother of the People." And she loved her children in return – although she sometimes grew jealous and resentful, sensing that they loved their father more. But still she owed them a debt of duty, though she also possessed a sense of entitlement as Empress. And at present Faustina felt entitled to either disagree with, or ignore, her husband's dull moralising.

"It's not about assigning blame, but rather finding a solution to the problem," Aurelius replied, wishing to placate rather than provoke his wife. He wanted to be the voice of reason – but since when did people listen to reason, especially in regards to their children?

"Well I think we can both agree that your continued absence will do little to solve the problem, as you see it. Your letters to Commodus, extolling the virtues of Plato or instructing him to devote himself to geometry rather than fencing, are poor compensation for you actually being here, engaging with your son. He needs deeds, not words," the woman pronounced, somewhat relishing the scenario of being able to chastise her philosopher-husband. Faustina proceeded to turn to face her mirror, tossing her head in doing so, and continued to brush her hair.

"You know that I have duties as Emperor."

"You also have duties as a father," Faustina replied, this time raising her voice and losing her composure a little – although her outburst also coincided with her hairbrush becoming snagged, which may have increased her frustration. The Empress regained her poise, however. "We need not consider Commodus' behaviour as a problem, but rather as a prospective virtue. He will be Emperor one day. Wilfulness and selfishness are part of the job description. He is just growing accustomed to ruling and getting his own way."

Aurelius first sighed, as if wanting to release any anger or anxiety from his body, and then took a deep breath as if he were about to make a long speech. Yet he merely sighed again, too tired to argue.

Marriage is an endless campaign… And there are always more defeats than triumphs.

Faustina sighed to herself too as she looked up at the simmering, low-cut gown hanging above her dresser. It was made from the finest Chinese silks. She loved the feel of the material on her stomach, breasts and thighs – caressing her like fingertips. *He* – Avidius – had bought the dress for her last year (although unbeknownst to Faustina Pollio Atticus had given the soldier the garment to make a gift of it to his lover). She wanted to wear the dress for him this evening, to have him undress her with his eyes. Yet her lover had met with her husband tonight instead of her, to talk about politics.

As much as Faustina, as a mother, could criticise Aurelius for being an absent father, she was glad of being able to live a separate life from her husband as a wife. *Absence may make the heart grow fonder but familiarity breeds contempt.* Living apart for most of the year had probably saved, rather than ruined, their marriage. Faustina recalled how they had had much to catch up on during her husband's first night back in the Imperial Palace. She had asked him about the war in the north and he had asked her about Commodus. They had slept together too, although she had considered that he had done so out of politeness. But by the following evening a familiar wall of silence had grown up between them both again. Neither was sure who had laid the first brick – and neither appeared to want to breach the wall now it was in place.

Aurelius climbed into bed. Perhaps he would pretend to fall asleep again before she joined him, Faustina thought – and hoped. The Empress finished brushing her hair and then began to clean the make-up off her face, before rubbing oil into her skin. Her back was turned to the bed but she occasionally glanced at her husband in the mirror, who had his back turned towards her. Occasionally she opened her legs slightly, tilted her head back and brushed her fingertips along and between her thighs. Her skin tingled as she imagined *him* touching her. She pictured his brooding looks, his strong jaw and cleft chin – which she would kiss and run her tongue over. They didn't make children in the bedroom, they made love. Faustina had taken many lovers over the years, but this affair was different. She believed that she loved Cassius. She remembered their last night together, how their sweat-glazed bodies had slotted against each other and how Cassius had promised he would take care of her and Commodus if anything happened to Aurelius. And he had meant it.

Yet Faustina would never leave her husband. She was the wife of the Emperor over the mistress of a soldier. She was the First Lady of Rome – and the Mother of the People could not abandon her children. She admired and was devoted to Marcus too – in her own way. She thought him intelligent, hard-working and just. He was a good man. *Too good.* His decency was construed as a weakness. Rome needs a Caesar, rather than Cicero, as its Emperor. She would sometimes shout and rail at him, but he would neither raise his hand nor voice in return. She occasionally wished he would – just to show some passion. *Be a man, rather than statue…*

As well as tingling for Cassius, Faustina felt twinges of guilt in regards to her husband. *He should take a mistress, either out of desire or revenge... He is probably the only faithful Emperor in the history of Rome... I want him to feel what I feel when I'm with Cassius – love and happiness...* Faustina thought how over the years numerous courtesans, young men and young wives had batted their eyes at the stoical Emperor, but he had merely rolled his eyes in reply. He took in little wine and ate simply. The only things he devoured were his books. *He looks more like the grandfather of his people now. More than love him, I pity him... He's too good – for this world.*

Marcus Aurelius pretended to be asleep. Rather than worrying about the future of his marriage he was thinking about Rufus Atticus' news – and the future of Rome. He tried to remain stoical, but couldn't.

19.

"Hold the line!" Atticus bellowed over the roar of the approaching enemy. At first the mercenaries had walked towards the line of legionaries, spitting out curses and looking to intimidate the soldiers through the weight of their numbers. But, twenty yards from their enemy, the snarling pack were let off the leash and ordered to attack the praetorians.

Spear tips and sword points quickly poked out from the front rank of shield wall. The soldiers gritted their teeth and gripped the sweat-soaked straps of their scutums, ready to stand firm against the first wave of men who would crash against their human dam.

Chen stood on top of one of his wagons to survey his battlefield, his face twisted in malice. The Chinaman had been surprised by the presence of the soldiers but he judged that the small contingent of praetorians could but delay, rather than defeat, his purpose. His men would punch through part of the shield wall, pour through the breach and then attack them from all sides. They could either retreat now, or die.

The second rank of legionaries stood as a buttress behind the first. The second and third ranks of mercenaries spurred the first on. Their lack of shields gave the praetorian's a distinct advantage, however, as the two forces met, like two rows of butting stags or rams. Atticus pushed his shield forward and stabbed, furiously and ferociously, at his enemies. His gladius was slick with blood immediately as it sliced through hands, thighs, shins and necks. A familiar cacophony of sounds reverberated in his eardrums – the clang of swords, blood-curdling screams and thousands of curses being traded to create a crescendo of hatred. Cudgels and short swords thumped upon his scutum. His men, to the left and right of him, similarly worked themselves up into a frenzied rhythm of carnage. Sword arms glistened with blood and gore. When they felled their enemies they swiftly stabbed them in the chest or face. A wounded man can still fight on, but a dead man can't. Atticus killed and injured more than most, looking to lead by example as well as just survive.

But still the enemy advanced. Hydra-headed.

*

"Pollio Atticus? I thought that I was the only one who was supposed to make house calls in the middle of the night. Are you ill?"

The statesman, accompanied by a couple of (armed) attendants, had entered Galen's ground floor laboratory. The smell of sulphur, tar and garum (from the physician's evening meal) filled Atticus' nostrils. The aristocrat turned his nose up as much at the décor as the pungent smells though. Instead of statues lining the walls Atticus took in all manner of ghastly looking stuffed animals. A half-eaten plate of food sat next to a half-dissected lamb. Various noxious liquids simmered away on a large table, which groaned under the weight of scientific apparatus.

"Politicians are not so different from doctors. I also stay up late and work tirelessly for the good of the people."

Galen couldn't quite tell in the half-light of the laboratory whether the senator's expression was unctuous or ironic.

"There are indeed perhaps a few similarities between our professions. Many politicians and doctors are overpaid – and many peddle false hope."

Galen remained seated at his desk at the end of the room, but stopped writing up his notes. He glanced nervously at the two menacing-looking attendants who had started to inspect and handle some of his equipment.

"You forgot to mention that we are also both akin to gods, doctor. When the people venture to the temple each day and pray for prosperity and good health are they not really supplicating us?"

"I'm not sure whether even *my* ego would permit me to call myself a god. Not even physicians live forever – and politicians more than most can suffer earthly changes in fortune."

"You are right, but changes in fortune can sometimes be for the better. As they have been today, when I heard that you had discovered a cure for the plague. You have saved the Empire Galen. For once the peoples' praise might match the esteem which you hold yourself in. Do you have the cure in your possession? Who else knows about it?"

"I am afraid that I have been sworn to secrecy," Galen said, shifting uncomfortably in his seat, his eyes flitting back and forth between the statesman and his bodyguards.

"That's a shame. Fortunately you seem to possess the right instruments to make you open up to us though – and to extract any secrets," Atticus replied, smiling with equanimity, as he casually picked up a surgical clamp and bone saw from the table next to him. "I'd prefer for you to cooperate Galen, rather than have to say to you in the morning, 'Physician, heal thyself'."

"I'm grateful for you reminding me of a fundamental difference between our two professions. A doctor gives an oath that he 'will do no harm'. I'm not sure if a politician could give such an oath, let alone keep it."

"You think you have an answer for everything, doctor. But what would you say if I cut your tongue out?" The senator loomed over the physician at his desk. Cruelty gleamed in his eyes like two polished gold coins.

I'll extract the truth from him or he'll take his secrets – and the cure – to the grave.

"I'd answer for him," Gaius Maximus remarked, appearing from out of the doorway situated behind the physician. The centurion had listened from a storeroom whilst he heard the statesman incriminate himself – but decided to intervene when he felt that Galen might be in danger. From what Rufus Atticus' messenger had reported it seemed that Claudia's testimony would be enough to convict Pollio Atticus of treason, but his presence at Galen's laboratory cemented his guilt further. Unfortunately Rufus had been right about his father.

The esteemed politician was, for once, lost for words when he witnessed the fearsome soldier standing before him. His features dropped, as if he had just been told that someone had died – or that his fortune had been lost at sea.

"I am afraid that you have been wrongly informed senator. I warrant that you will have more chance of finding the shield of Achilles, or the Golden Fleece, upon that dissected lamb over there, than the cure for the plague here tonight in this the laboratory. Much like the idea of an honest politician, the cure doesn't exist. There, see, and you didn't even have to torture me to discover the truth," Galen said, enjoying the moment. The enemy of his friend had been defeated.

Half a dozen stern-faced legionaries followed Maximus out of the storeroom, ready to apprehend their quarry. Pollio Atticus grimaced, baring his teeth like a cornered wild animal.

"It seems that the spider has been caught up in his own web," Maximus remarked, little masking the antagonism he felt towards the enemy of the state. "Or rather you've been caught up in a web of your own son's making. Rufus knew that you would be tempted by the prize of a cure to the plague. He also rightly judged that you would use your own daughter to glean information out of me. There are beasts which devour their own offspring that have treated their children better than you have yours. But Claudia has finally taken her revenge and betrayed you. I've ordered a number of my men to search your study. I expect that they will uncover evidence of bribery and propaganda. No amount of dinner parties will be able to buy you favours and influence now."

Pollio Atticus glowered, unblinkingly, at the low-born but arrogant centurion. *Aurelius' lap-dog.* Resentment powered his heart and thoughts. He had been betrayed by his own family – the people who he had spent his life trying to protect and better. They could now burn and starve with the rest of Rome.

"You should take consolation from the fact that you will do that which even Cicero failed to do as a statesman, namely unite the classes. Senators, soldiers, merchants and plebs alike will all want to see you strung up for your crimes – and watch the crows feast upon you from the feet up. I may even request what's left of you, to dissect as a medical specimen. At least in death you may prove to be of some positive use to Rome."

"The crows will have plenty to feast on after this evening, doctor, don't worry. If you wish to do no harm to Rome, then you will have to do no harm to me. The Emperor will soon discover that I am of more use to the capital alive than dead," Pollio Atticus said, regaining some of his confidence, believing that he could still escape prosecution. *Aurelius is weak... He will need my grain reserves. He will negotiate...*

"I take it that you're referring to your plan to destroy the grain surplus? Rufus is in the process of dealing with your band of mercenaries as we speak. But even if your Chinaman succeeds in burning down the granary I'm sure that I can make Pollux open up, to use your phrase, and tell me where he is storing the grain that you have recently purchased from the east," Maximus said, thinking how, as much as he was enjoying apprehending the statesman, he would rather be fighting alongside his friend. *I am a soldier rather than spy.*

Pollio Atticus momentarily mused that if Chen encountered his son at the wharf then he would kill him – and he knew not if he should feel pleasure or pain at the prospect of his son/enemy dying.

"You think that you have won – and thought of everything? Yet come the morning, centurion, you will feel a stronger sense of regret and remorse than I," Atticus announced, forebodingly.

Before Maximus had time to draw any meaning from the senator's words he was called upon to draw his sword. Pollio Atticus, realising that his capture would lead to his death, glanced at his two attendants and nodded his head – subtly commanding them to attack and aid his escape. *Desperate times call for desperate measures.* Atticus turned and ran towards the door at the other end of the laboratory, where he had originally entered. The two bodyguards filled the space he vacated and stood between their master and the praetorian.

Rather than just looking to stand guard and buy the statesman time to retreat the larger of the attendants took the fight to his enemy. His muscular forearms were covered with a number of tattoos of small swords, signifying kills in the arena from his time as a gladiator. He charged forward like a bull with his large shoulders rolling – and his head down. Maximus reacted quickly and threw a ceramic beaker at his assailant. The beaker smashed against his forehead and a roar of anger swiftly turned into a howl of pain. The bovine, tattooed attendant lost concentration – without losing momentum – and when he regained his senses he found that the centurion was about to punch his gladius into his sternum. Even Galen winced as he heard the sound of the blade scrape against bone.

The bull had been slain. Maximus raised his legs and kicked the body away from him, freeing his sword.

The second bodyguard, his wiry body twitching with unreleased energy and hatred, stood his ground rather than attacking the soldier. Two triangular bronze blades from the daggers he wielded glinted in the yellow light from the oil lamps hanging over him. In order to distract his opponent, to grant more time for his master to escape or to intimidate the centurion, the bodyguard commenced to skilfully twirl the knives around in his hands. Maximus merely rolled his eyes in response to the display, however, out of boredom and contempt. He turned his head, nodded to one of his legionaries to toss him the javelin he was holding – and a few moments later skewered his enemy.

Pollio Atticus walked around the corpse of his attendant as a brace of legionaries, who had been covering the front entrance to the house, led the statesman back towards Maximus.

"It looks like you'll have to now hire another couple of bodyguards, as well as a good advocate," the centurion drily remarked, whilst his thoughts turned again to how his former optio was faring at the wharf.

Hold the line.

20.

The tang of blood and sewerage from the river swirled around in the night air. Rufus Atticus' sword arm ached – and felt numb – as if it were one large bruise hanging from his shoulder. Although his throat felt increasing sore Atticus still offered up words of encouragement to his men, in between trying to catch his breath. Thankfully, at last, there was a respite in the fighting. The front ranks of the enemy drew back. Once bitten, twice shy. Only half of the mercenaries facing them found the will to jeer at the legionaries now. A line of corpses was strewn across the street and acted as an effective barricade for the shield wall. They would have to step over their fallen comrades to get to their enemy now. Just surviving felt tantamount to a victory at the moment for the outnumbered soldiers, but Atticus knew that the only thing that he had won so far was time. But for now that was enough.

The centurion instructed his men in the second rank to trade places with the wounded in the first rank – and offered up a silent prayer to Apollo to save them all.

"Not one step back," Chen commanded, gnashing his teeth, but such was his frustration and ire that he did so, unconsciously, in his native language. Back in his homeland the first rank would have been ordered to fall upon the enemy's swords, in order for the subsequent ranks to advance. As if in sympathy with the Chinaman the mule, pulling the wagon he was standing on, screeched in complaint and confusion. Chen took consolation whilst he seethed, however. He would soon be rid of praetorian gadflies, having sent a contingent of men around the backstreets to come out and attack the shield wall from behind. They would be trapped in a press, but instead of olive oil blood would ooze out. But there must be blood soon, he thought, conscious of the time. If these praetorians were aware of his force's presence then others were doubtless being mobilised – and Chen had no wish to be trapped between a burning warehouse and small army of legionaries once he had set the building alight.

The barge bobbed gently up and down on the river. Cassius Bursus attuned his body to its rhythms – and took account of its movements for when he would unleash his arrows... And at last a target had come into sight. A wagon carrying barrels of oil stopped close to the riverside (instead of being hidden among a group of the enemy). Apollo lovingly stroked his bow, strengthened and decorated with horn, out of habit and superstition. He nocked a shaft and ordered a young legionary to light him – and the rest of the archers – up.

Make every arrow count.

The fifty or so men that Chen had ordered to attack the irksome shield wall from behind finally appeared from the mouth of a street across the way from the soldiers – and began to form up. They launched into a united roar, or jeer, partly to intimidate the legionaries – but more so to announce to their comrades that they could soon coordinate their offensives. Somewhat out of breath though, from having raced through the backstreets, the small force slowly – but menacingly – marched towards the thin red line of Roman shields.

"Second rank, about face," Rufus Atticus commanded, making his voice heard above all manner of other sounds. "Nothing has changed. We still need to just hold the line. We can and will fight on two fights, as Caesar did at Alesia – and these bastards before us now seem about as courageous as Gauls too, no? A relief force is on its way." Or rather two relief forces, the centurion hoped. Atticus possessed more confidence in his tone than he did in his heart, but that was part of the brief of being an officer, he considered.

Both groups of mercenaries, either side of the lines of legionaries, raised their weapons aloft to signal to each other that they were ready to attack and trap their enemy in a fatal vice.

Atticus wiped the blade of his gladius on the skirt of his tunic. Many of the soldiers looked more like butchers than praetorians. Fear froze a few jaws and knuckles cracked, as men gripped their shields and swords once more. They would fight on – and not just because retreating or surrendering were no longer options. They would fight on, for their own survival, for the man standing next to them, and for the glory of Rome – and in that order, Atticus judged. He had a letter that would go to Maximus, to help sort out his affairs, should he not survive the night. He told himself that he had been in more perilous situations and lived to tell the tale, but he was at pains to remember exactly when those situations were. He briefly remembered *her*. He always believed that he would see Sara again, in this world or the next. The philosophical soldier offered up a prayer to the gods to either let him live or let him find peace in the next life – and remembered his Socrates: *Death may be the greatest of all human blessings.*

*

Chen licked his lips in anticipation of the imminent massacre. His only regret was that his own sword would remain unbloodied, as he surveyed the encounter from the rear. The mercenaries lowered their arms as the signal to attack, but at the same time Apollo and his small force of a dozen or so archers launched their volley of fire arrows into the barrels of oil. Not all of the missiles hit their mark, but enough did. And the first volley was quickly followed up with a second. The large, sharpened, burning arrowheads cracked open the casks and set their contents alight. Bright yellow flames slashed through the inky night, covering the wagon and the men surrounding the vehicle. Globules of burning oil spat out in all directions. The rearing and charging mules did much to spread the fire and create chaos. A few of the mercenaries rightly hacked one of the animals to death, inspiring others to do so as well.

Panic and confusion ensued, each fuelling the other. The main attack on the line of legionaries stalled as the mercenaries turned their heads to look backwards rather than forwards. A few believed that fire was raining down upon them from the gods, protecting the capital. The fire sowed disorder and as men scattered to avoid the flames another target opened up to Apollo's archers – and they targeted the wagon accordingly. The fire spread like a plague. The highly flammable oil set light to anything it came in contact with – timber, clothes and skin. Rivulets of flames ran in between the cobble stones. Another wagon erupted, spewing out flames like a mini volcano. A few of the mercenaries were trampled underfoot – and burned alive. Smoke began to belch out from the conflagration and choke the enemy too. The fire arrows which missed the targets of the wagons hissed and thudded into necks, chests and faces. The smell of burning flesh, as well as burning oil, began to singe nostrils. Some, fearing that they could be trapped by the fire retreated or jumped into the river.

Chen's eyes were ablaze and his rage burned as hotly as the fire. His mission, rather the grain warehouse, was turning into ash.

Atticus again ordered his men to hold the line. As tempted as some were to use the distraction and destruction of the fire as an opportunity to escape – or even counter-attack the enemy –

the centurion realised that they should still just retain their defensive position.

Free from the threat of the fire – and the contingent of archers on the barge – the mercenaries positioned on the warehouse side of the battle decided to continue their attack. Their blood was up – and the offensive might spur their comrades on to similarly engage the enemy. The Roman shield wall would break, as soon as it was pressured from both sides. Yet the encirclers were about to be encircled.

As well as sending messengers to the Emperor and Maximus earlier Atticus had also sent a young legionary off to his old friend Milo, the landlord at *The Trojan Pig*. The tavern would be inhabited by various ex-soldiers, dockers, guild members and boisterous drunks. It was their city as much as his – and Atticus had asked Milo to mobilise as many men as he could to bolster his forces. They would be rewarded with gold, as well as a sense of pride.

Some looked as if they had already been in a fight that night – and had lost: scar-faced, haggard and glassy-eyed. Some were armed with short swords and clubs but others carried carpentry hammers, bread knives, rocks and clay jugs. They were all fuelled, however, with a belly full of wine and a sense of patriotism. They walked towards the line of mercenaries in a loose, but purposeful formation. Atticus offered up a salute to Milo. The landlord, who had recruited his rag-tag army from his own tavern and a couple of neighbouring establishments, gave a curse-filled order to attack. A handful of mercenaries at the end of the line escaped while they still could. But the would-be victors now became victims as they were caught between the praetorians and the tavern brawlers. Blood splattered the cobblestones. Legionaries stabbed, sliced and eviscerated. Retreat and surrender were not an option. Howls of rage and agony both spiralled up into the air, like the nearby tongues of fire. A skull was stoved in by a water jug. It was a massacre, but not the one Chen had envisioned. Soldiers and citizens out-swore and out-fought the band of cynical mercenaries.

By the time the legionaries and Milo's men had slaughtered the last of their opponents over half of Chen's forces had retreated, routed by fire and fear. Atticus finally breathed out, believing the worst to be over. Sweat began to pour down his face from the furnace-like heat of the burning wagons – and corpses. He offered up a prayer of thanks to Apollo. He would have his men advance, in formation, but he would allow them to catch their breath first.

"Good job, Sir," Gneaus Casca, a grizzled veteran of campaigns in both Egypt and Germany, expressed whilst standing next to his centurion, nodding in appreciation at his officer. Casca was a descendant of the famous legionary Tiro Casca, who had fought alongside Julius Caesar and Maximus' antecedent, Lucius Oppius – the Sword of Rome. "You held the line."

"No, Gnaeus, we all held the line," Atticus replied, warmly clasping Casca on the shoulder – thinking how the veteran's approval meant more to him than a dozen medals.

*

"If I can see the weaknesses opening up throughout the Empire, you can be sure that our enemies can see them too… If Aurelius cannot stem the tide against corruption, the tribes of the north, and the plague then how do you think his wastrel son will fare when he comes to power? Rather than stem the tide we will all drown in a flood. The Empire will fall. A golden age will turn to rust…In restraining me, you are shackling progress." A proud, but defeated, Pollio Atticus carped on as a legionary bound his hands and feet with rope. Partly Maximus had wanted to restrain Atticus to prevent him from trying to escape again – but more so he wished to humiliate the self-important statesman and treat him like a common criminal. He envisioned him being locked up for years, like Vercingetorix – only seeing daylight on the day of his execution.

The centurion turned a deaf ear to the disgraced politician's protestations. He spoke instead to Galen, in order to convince the doctor that it may not be safe for him to remain in his house. It would be better for him to spend the night in the Imperial Palace, where Maximus could guarantee his safety. At first Galen was dismissive of the soldier's fears but eventually Maximus won the argument (it was perhaps the first time he, or anyone, had won an argument with the doctor).

After Galen had collected some things – and attended to a number of his experiments in his laboratory – they were ready to leave. Just as they were about to so, however, a breathless red-haired legionary, Horatius, rushed in. Maximus had sent the soldier to Aurelia's house earlier, in order to inform her that it was unlikely that he would be home that evening. Despite the strangeness of the scene – the restrained statesman and unfamiliar scientific equipment – the dutiful Horatius made a direct line for his centurion. His expression was pale, disturbed. He tried to compose himself before he spoke, but couldn't. He was unable to look his officer squarely in the eye, like he had been drilled to do when delivering a message or orders. Horatius leaned into the officer, gently laid a hand on his shoulder, and whispered something into his ear. As he did so Maximus looked like his legs might give way from underneath him. His fingers dug into the table like talons to prop himself up. The soldier's face first screwed itself up, as if it were about to collapse upon itself in grief – but then became a picture, a paragon, of anger. But anger was overthrown by sorrow again, as Horatius finished his whispered report. A couple of tears streamed down Maximus' cheek – and he seemed dead to the world.

All present were mystified by the exchange and intrigued by the news the centurion could have received from the young soldier, except Pollio Atticus – who now more than ever gave off the appearance of a condemned man. The politician attempted to look innocent when the centurion glanced in his direction, but for once he failed to do so.

Maximus calmly walked towards the prisoner, drew his sword and plunged the blade into Pollio Atticus' throat. Blood sprayed and gurgled from the fatal wound. Maximus grabbed the statesman's toga and briefly held him up, wanting to look him in the eye as the light, and life, was extinguished from his aspect. He then let the body slump to the ground. The centurion's expression seemed just as detached and lifeless as that of the corpse at his feet. Without a word, ignoring his duties and the people around him, the blood-strewn soldier proceeded to walk away. No one thought to try and apprehend the murderer of the prisoner. Galen, after recovering from the shock of what he had just witnessed, pursued his friend out of the house. But Maximus was nowhere to be seen. The night had already swallowed him up.

21.

There was a hypnotic beauty to the reflection of the swirling, amber blaze in the Tiber. But the reality, behind the reflection, was far uglier and deadlier. Timber from the wagons crackled and corpses sizzled. Smoke blackened all, a chorus of coughs sang out throughout the street and men shielded their faces from the intense heat. Blood and fire. The scene felt like Hades on earth, Rufus Atticus thought. The acrid smell – and gruesome sight – of a mule's eyeball burning (whilst the rest of its head remained untouched) made a young legionary retch. Atticus heard Gnaeus Casca describe the aftermath as being like a "charred charnel house".

Atticus and his men moved forward, and were met with little resistance. The battle was won. The task was to secure the peace. Surrender was now an option for the enemy, although those uninjured preferred to retreat and escape. The centurion tasked Milo and his men to make sure that the fire did not spread to the buildings facing the river. The promise of more gold spurred them on in their civic duty. He also asked Milo to attend to the wounded. Some of his men were beyond saving though. The next river they would be crossing would be the Styx, rather than Tiber. But they would mourn their fallen comrades later. There was work still to be done.

Earlier in the battle, after Chen had sensed that the tide was turning in the favour of the praetorians, he had raced towards the rear of his army in order to prevent the beginnings of a retreat. He had drawn his sword, bellowed out orders to advance and threatened his men – and he had even killed a couple of deserters to make an example of them – but not even the Chinaman could hold back the waters of defeat. The blaze had raged on and the mercenaries routed. One of his lieutenants had reported that the force, who were due to ambush the shield war from behind, had themselves been ambushed and overwhelmed. Chen had again let out a curse in his native language and had vowed that he would hunt down and kill whoever had betrayed his master. If guarded by Hercules himself Chen would still torture and terminate the traitor. When his lieutenant reported that the centurion commanding the enemy was their master's son the Chinaman was possessed by only one thought: *Kill him*.

Chen swam against the stream, heading in the opposite direction to the dishonourable curs of his men. His body firmed up beneath his blood and oil-soaked tunic. His skin glowed orange as he grew closer to the flames – and seemingly walked through them. He reached up and fingered a small piece of jade which hung around his neck. His father had given him the talisman as a reward for his first kill, at the age of fourteen. Out of superstition and habit he touched the stone every time he was about to kill someone.

The Chinaman drew his curved, polished sword and swiped the air with a flick of his wrist, cutting a path through the grey clouds of smoke.

Rufus Atticus was at the vanguard of his men. Flanked by two legionaries he moved forward, sidestepping corpses and puddles of flames. He passed a wagon, which had been turned sideways, half blocking the street. When he passed the vehicle flames spurted up and set light to a patch of oil, which ran along the other side of the street – causing a wall of fire which cut him off from the rest of his men. Atticus had little time to take in the situation, however, as the two legionaries beside him advanced to engage the solitary swordsman standing before them.

The Chinaman wore a deranged look on his face, as if drunk or drugged. He barked out something in a barbaric tongue and then spat out an insult, directed at the centurion, which the legionaries comprehended not but seemed to contain the word "honour" or "dishonour".

The first legionary felt a rush of blood and ran and slashed at the enemy in one movement. Chen gracefully avoided the attack and deftly sliced his opponent's forearm, disarming him. The last thing the soldier heard was his gladius clang on the ground, before the tip of the Chinaman's sword sliced open his jugular vein.

The second legionary understandably approached the barbarian with more caution, crouching behind his large shield. Despite the leather-faced veteran's wealth of experience in combat he was unsure of his strategy in dealing with the mercenary, who had bested his comrade with such poise and savagery. Before the soldier had a chance to settle upon a plan of attack though the assassin lunged forward with his body and sword in one motion and punctured both the legionary's shield and abdomen.

The centurion briefly closed his eyes in remorse – he had lost two more men, needlessly, after the battle was over. His eyes burned with scorn, however, when he opened them again.

Kill him.

Flames whipped up in the air behind the Chinaman. His face was streaked in sweat and spotted with blood. His cruel mouth twisted itself into a crueller smile as he glowered at the soldier. Atticus thought how Chen could have come from Hades, having been spat back out.

"Who betrayed our plans?" Chen demanded, rather than asked.

The centurion remained resolutely silent. *If I don't kill him, he'll kill Claudia.* He dropped his shield, believing that it could prove a cumbersome hindrance in combating the agile Chinaman, and swished his sword around in his hand, loosening up his wrist and arm. He was conscious of the throwing dagger he still possessed on the back of his belt – but was also conscious of how agile his father's bodyguard was.

"If you don't want to talk, that's fine. I'll be happy to cut the answers out of you."

Atticus approached his enemy; his men, shouting behind a wall of fire, spoke for him.

"Stick him, Sir… Kill the bastard…"

The legionaries rated their officer as one of the best swordsman in the barracks, perhaps even quicker and more skilful than Maximus, but the foreign mercenary was an unknown quantity. A couple of soldiers readied their javelins to try and spear the enemy, should it look like their centurion was doomed. The shot would be difficult through all the flames and smoke, however.

Chen's speed – and the superior length of his blade – put Atticus on the back foot immediately. The best the soldier could do at present was just parry his opponent's attacks, which seemed to come from all angles; there wasn't any time to recover and launch counter-attacks. A song of swords rang out over the background of the snarling fire. Thankfully there were breaks in Chen's offensives. The assassin commenced to circle and prowl around his enemy before launching swift, brief sorties – a predator, toying with his prey. But Atticus hoped that confidence would breed over-confidence. If he could momentarily distract or decentre the Chinaman he might have a chance to make his throwing dagger count.

"Tell me, does my father house you with his slaves, or his pets? He spoke to me about you once. He says you were always eager to please, like a woman – or bitch…"

Chen's next attack was more ferocious, but less clinical. He was also more breathless and less in control of himself when he spoke.

"I'm going to gut you like an animal – and make you scream like a woman."

"But you'll still be you and I'll still be me," Atticus replied, unable (and unwilling) to mask his superiority and amusement in relation to his father's bodyguard.

Chen paused as a raw resentment welled up inside his chest – and a certain self-realisation dawned upon his face. Atticus sensed his opportunity. He would be throwing the knife with his weaker arm, but it had been strong enough in the past. His left hand crept behind his back but then unleashed itself like a ballista. The blade was aiming for Chen's right ribs but Chen quickly turned his body and brought his sword across, deflecting the dagger away. The assassin flared his nostrils and was angry at himself, as well as the soldier, for his opponent nearly besting him. There would be no respite now.

Kill him.

The flurry of lunges and slices came thicker and faster than before. He had felt safer earlier when being attacked by scores of mercenaries as he stood in the shield wall, compared to the threat of his current, solitary, opponent. Chen moved relentless forward and Atticus retreated. His back was soon pressed against the plaster wall of the building which looked out onto the Tiber. The centurion flinched as his head nearly struck an arrow, still burning and lodged in a wooden shutter. Exhaustion – and the assassin's skill – told. Chen increased, rather than diminished, the power of his attacks. He eventually knocked the soldier's gladius from his hand. Atticus gazed at his enemy with a mixture of defeat and defiance. Rufus noted earlier that some of his men had their javelins still in their hands, ready to cut down the mercenary. But even if they had a will to do so their view of Chen was now obscured by the burning wagon and haze of smoke.

"Feel free to come back and haunt me when you die centurion. That way you can watch me when I cut off the head of your friend Maximus."

Chen sniggered after speaking. The tip of his sword hung cruelly under Atticus' left eye. He could smell the garlic on the Chinaman's breath and the oil on his clothes.

"You'll see the fires of Hades before me," the Roman replied – and grabbed the flaming arrow next to him and tossed it against his enemy's chest. For a moment it looked like Chen wore a breastplate of gold. But it also looked like he would still run Atticus through, as he drew back his sword – ready to stab the centurion. But the Chinaman's tunic was too heavily doused in oil. Tongues of fire quickly licked his throat and then his face. For once the fearless assassin howled in fear and agony. His screams cut through the night air like a bolt of lightning. Atticus hurriedly gave the human torch a wide berth. Chen dropped his sword and attempted to beat the flames out with his hands – but his hands duly caught on fire. When he fell to the ground and rolled around in attempt to extinguish the flames he rolled around in oil. His skin blistered. The Chinaman writhed and stretched out his body – and then doubled-up into a ball. But the screaming didn't stop. The fire ate into his cheeks and eyes. The centurion was tempted to pick up his enemy's sword and put him out of his misery. But, for once, Rufus Atticus refused to give into temptation.

*

Earlier in the evening Chen had cut through arteries and veins, so blood had both gushed and oozed out of Aurelia's body. Blood could be found on her bedclothes, the flowers on her desk, the tiled floor and the mosaics and paintings on the wall depicting scenes from Virgil's Idylls.

Pollio Atticus had ordered his bodyguard to murder the woman, in order to exact his revenge against Maximus. He would make him suffer – and then have him killed. An agent of the statesman had reported how close the officer was to Aurelia. Atticus not only wanted to pay the soldier back for thwarting his plans three years ago, before the Battle of Pannonia, but for stealing his son away from him. The officer had introduced his son to Aurelius – and Pollio considered him to be the reason why his son was now loyal to the Emperor rather than his own father. Pollio Atticus always settled his debts, in his favour.

Chen, accompanied by a quartet of trusted men, had forced his way into the house. No explanations were given, no words were uttered, as the staff were slaughtered. *Dead men tell no tales*. Aurelia and Helena had run up to Aurelia's bedroom and had tried to escape out of the window. But Chen had discovered them. He had been tempted to give the pretty serving girl to his men, as a prize. But time was precious, so he had stabbed her through the mid-rift and let her bleed to death. Chen had been more meticulous and imaginative when it came to killing Aurelia, however, as his master had ordered. He had first beat any resistance out of her. He had then clinically sliced open her hamstrings, breasts and face. "I want him to barely recognise her... Make her suffer, so he'll suffer," Pollio Atticus had remarked, whilst casually rearranging the folds in his toga.

Aurelia's last thoughts had been a prayer to God, for Maximus.

By the time Maximus had reached the house and found Aurelia her corpse had stiffened. He first properly covered up her naked, bloody body. Her face was horribly disfigured but he still held her in his arms and kissed her forehead, rocking her as if she, or he, were a distressed child. He frequently smeared himself in her blood, trying to wipe the tears from his eyes. Rage and remorse hammered upon his heart, alternating their blows.

As Maximus finally got up to leave, his hand now gripping his sword rather than cradling her head, he noticed the gold band on Aurelia's bedside table. It was the ring, back from the engravers, that she was intending to give him. He read the inscription, written on the inside of the band.

The light shines in the darkness.

*

The legionaries clapped the archers on the back and hailed them as heroes as they reached dry land again, though the archers felt the infantryman were the heroes for fighting in the shield wall against such superior numbers. Banter and roars of laughter could now be heard over the roar of the receding blaze. They would all be drinking and swapping stories long into the night – and morning. Milo would open the good stuff too and either lower the prices of his wine or whores – but not both.

Spray still freckled Apollo's brow as he made his way through the crowd of jubilant soldiers. The tension only left his features, however, when he spied his centurion. The archer recognised a palpable relief in Atticus' expression too, little realising how much of that relief was due to being alive, rather than winning his first battle as a commander. The two friends met and shook hands.

"You've helped save Rome. They'll be a host of senators wanting to have dinner with you now, rather than just their wives," Apollo joked.

"I didn't save Rome alone," the centurion replied, looking on the men around him with a sense of pride and gratitude. "Thank you for making your arrows count."

"Well, if I'm honest, I didn't make them all count. One went wayward I think and just struck some shutters on one of the buildings."

"That one counted too, don't worry," Atticus said, beaming with wry amusement. He also smiled due to the realisation that he had one less burdensome decision to make as a centurion – that of choosing his optio.

Epilogue

The afternoon sky was fretted with a lattice-work of snow-white clouds. The copper rays of the sun bleached the stone and plaster walls of the bustling, expansive city. The fires from the street battle had long died out, indeed there was little or no evidence of a battle ever having taken place a few nights ago. Rome was Rome again, normalcy reigned – for nearly everyone.

The roles were somewhat reversed when Galen encountered Rufus Atticus in the garden of the Imperial Palace. The usually po-faced doctor offered the centurion a consoling smile, while the often amused soldier remained disconsolate. The doctor was taking his leave from sitting with the Emperor, as Atticus arrived.

Marcus Aurelius sat on a chair on the lawn, wearing a sunhat akin to the kind that Octavius Caesar had worn as a boy and man. The Emperor took off the hat, however, to take in the centurion. His eyes were red-rimmed with drink and sleeplessness, or both. His mouth was uncharacteristically downturned. His gait was as heavy as his heart. Although Atticus had washed his tunic since the battle it was still stained with blood and smelled of smoke.

"Please Rufus, sit down. I take it that you haven't heard anything from Maximus?"

"No. No one has."

After saying goodbye to Aurelia Maximus had gone back to the barracks, collected his personal belongings and disappeared. He had, however, left a letter each for Atticus and the Emperor, which largely expressed the same sentiments.

"The army and the Empire have had their pound of flesh out of me… Treat me like I'm a dead man. Don't try and look for me. All you'll find is the ghost of someone I used to be… I have valued your friendship over the years; if you have valued mine then leave me be…"

"And how are you Rufus?"

"The art of living is more like wrestling than dancing," the centurion evenly replied, quoting a maxim that the Emperor had once shared with him.

"And how are you wrestling with the fact that you were right, in regards to your suspicions about your father?" Aurelius refrained from asking how Atticus felt about his best friend having killed his father.

"Galen may not have found a remedy to the plague, but Rome has at least been cured of another disease this week," Atticus answered, matter-of-factly.

"And how is your sister?"

The Emperor judged that Claudia's confession had helped prevent her father's mercenaries from burning down the grain warehouse. Atticus had failed to mention in his report how she had confessed not in order to save Rome, but to try and save Maximus. Aurelius had spared her from prosecution and, fearing for her safety from any of her father's agents who may wish to take their revenge, he offered her the use of one of his country estates to reside in. She had agreed to leave Rome, under the proviso that her husband would not be allowed to join her. Claudia had also insisted on paying for Aurelia's funeral. Her parting from her brother had been strained. Much had remained unsaid, on both sides.

"She will be fine," Atticus replied, lying. Claudia had discovered that she had a heart – only for it to be broken.

Aurelius was neither convinced by the centurion's words or by his demeanour. Atticus reminded Aurelius of himself, when he had mentioned to his wife that all would be well with Commodus.

"I'm pleased. You must feel free to take some leave and visit her, before we journey north again."

"Have you decided Maximus' fate?"

As seemingly abrupt as Atticus' question was Aurelius had expected that the centurion would ask it, sooner rather than later. Maximus was now a deserter, one who had murdered a prisoner in cold blood – against the express wishes of his Emperor. Also, Aurelius had declined to tell Atticus that within two days of Maximus disappearing a number of his father's agents had been found brutally murdered. The Emperor had asked Galen to carry out autopsies on the bodies and concluded that the victims had been killed by an army issue gladius.

"As you may well have heard, Rufus, there are notable personages calling for me to condemn Maximus' actions, deem him a fugitive from justice and capture him. To make Maximus stand trial, and execute him. Occasionally politicians smell blood – whether mine or Maximus'. Antonius Reburrus, Julius Porticus and Gnaeus Varro – they are all getting on their moral high horses and calling for Maximus' head. I pray that sooner or later those self-same moral high horses trample them underfoot. They have been arguing that centurions, or friends of the Emperor, should not be above the law. I dare say that they would like politicians – and their friends – to remain above the law though.

'Should I give into their calls and prosecute Maximus then I will earn the opprobrium of the Praetorian Guard, or indeed the entire army. Instead of preventing a riot the Guard may well cause one, should I hang Maximus out to dry. As you may well imagine, Rufus, I have been mulling over my options. I would rather have to answer the big philosophical problems, such as discern the nature of the gods or articulate what is the good life. I barely slept last night – not because I was worrying about my dilemma, but rather from trying to find a solution to it. Ironically, in such similar instances before, I would have consulted Maximus. Yet I realised that I still could – and that he had unwittingly provided me with a solution to square the circle and avoid upsetting either the Senate or the Guard – although neither may be entirely happy with the imminent outcome regarding Maximus' fate.

'Sometime in the near future Galen will discover a corpse and judge it to be that of the hero – and fugitive – Gaius Maximus. The face will be sufficiently disfigured, either from a flesh wound or fire, but Galen's word will be trusted. Maximus asked us to treat him like a dead man, so let us grant our friend his last request. I was reading Plutarch the other day Rufus and I came across the line, 'Nothing so befits a ruler as the work of justice'. I'm not sure that I am doing right by Maximus, in relation to the letter of Roman law, but I hope that I am being just. For true justice is mercy, I believe."

For the first time since finding out about Maximus, Aurelia and his father, Rufus Atticus' face lit up in a smile.

The light shines in the darkness, and the darkness comprehends it not.

End Note

Although I often hang the plots of my books on the historical pegs of various battles or incidents from Ancient History *Sword of Empire: Centurion* is, more than usual, a work of fiction. I hope however the book has whetted your appetite to find out more about the period and Marcus Aurelius. If so I can recommended *Marcus Aurelius: Warrior, Philosopher, Emperor*. So too there is *The Antonines* by Michael Grant and *Marcus Aurelius: A Biography* by Anthony R. Birley. Essential reading also comes in the form, of course, of *The Meditations* by Marcus Aurelius.

Once again thank you to all of those readers who have been in touch over the past few years. I can be contacted via richard@sharpebooks.com and also @rforemanauthor on twitter.

Gaius Maximus and Rufus Atticus will return in *Sword of Empire: Emperor*.

Richard Foreman.

For submissions to *Sharpe Books* please contact Richard
Foreman richard@sharpebooks.com

Also by Richard Foreman

Warsaw

A Hero of Our Time

Sword of Rome Series
Sword of Rome: Standard Bearer
Sword of Rome: Alesia
Sword of Rome: Gladiator
Sword of Rome: Rubicon
Sword of Rome: Pharsalus
Sword of Rome: The Complete Campaigns
Swords of Rome: Omnibus of the Historical Series Books 1-3

Sword of Empire Series
Sword of Empire: Praetorian
Sword of Empire: Centurion
Sword of Empire: The Complete Campaigns
Sword of Empire: Omnibus

Raffles Series
Raffles: The Gentleman Thief
Raffles: Bowled Over
Raffles: A Perfect Wicket
Raffles: Caught Out
Raffles: Stumped
Raffles: Playing On
Raffles: Omnibus of Books 1 - 3
Raffles: The Complete Innings

Raffles: Complete Innings Boxset

Band of Brothers Series
Band of Brothers: The Complete Campaigns
Band of Brothers: Agincourt
Band of Brothers: The Game's Afoot
Band of Brothers: Omnibus
Band of Brothers: Harfleur

Augustus Series
Augustus: Son of Rome
Augustus: Son of Caesar

Pat Hobby Series
Pat Hobby's Last Shot
The Complete Pat Hobby
The Great Pat Hobby
The Return of Pat Hobby

*

Printed in Great Britain
by Amazon

37693142R00080